Hide and Shriek

by Tim Kelly

Baker's Plays
7611 Sunset Blvd.
Los Angeles, CA 90042
bakersplays.com

CHARACTERS
(In order of speaking)

GRANNY DIMSHROUD . . . . a mountain crone
AESOP . . . . her great-grandson
ADA DIMSHROUD . . . . Aesop's mother
JUNE HUNGERFORD . . . . worried young woman
from the city
ULYSSES DIMSHROUD . . . . Ada's husband
BETTY HUNGERFORD . . , ... June's older sister
MIKE HYDE . . . . graduate student hiking through the hills
WIDOW MURK . . . . no-nonsense neighbor
RUTH SPAULDING . . . . attorney
PAUL PEMBROOK . . . . landscape painter
SHERIFF GREEN . . . . lawman
ISABEL WARD . . . . college student
DORIS FINLEY* . . . . another
EDWINA HYDE . . . . young woman with a violent temper

The character of Doris can be switched to a male role, if desired --
DUKE.

SYNOPSIS

The action of the play takes place in an old house somewhere
in the Ozark Mountains. The time is the present.

ACT ONE
Scene 1: A summer night
Scene 2: One week later
Scene 3: That night

ACT TWO
Scene 1: Following day
Scene 2: Later

HIDE AND SHRIEK

ACT I SCENE 1

(*SETTING: The parlor of a rambling country house. Well over a hundred years old and looks it. Cobwebs everywhere. In its prime the house might have been handsome in a quaint sort of way, but the declining years have not been kind. Shabby and neglected, it seems to retain the original furnishings -- or what's left of them. A battered settee or sofa DOWN RIGHT CENTER. A round table with two chairs and crude stool DOWN LEFT CENTER. DOWN RIGHT is a cellar door. Key in the lock. STAGE RIGHT there's a fireplace with a bench in front. Box for wood LEFT of fireplace. Above the fireplace mantel is the portrait of a dour-looking 19th Century gentleman. This is Fowler "Mudslide" Dimshroud. UP RIGHT there's the entrance to a hallway that leads to the OFFSTAGE front door. UP RIGHT there's a table with a lamp. Another table and lamp UP LEFT CENTER. UPSTAGE CENTER there's an archway that leads into a small hall. Stairs to the second story LEFT in hallway. UP LEFT there are narrow French doors that are nearly always open. Below the French doors is a desk with a lamp. The entrance into the dining room, with the kitchen beyond, is below the desk. Rocking chair DOWN LEFT. To these "basics" should be added assorted atmospheric touches -- grandfather clock, an ancient carpet or rug(s), a rustic chandelier, framed family photographs. Some stuffed animal heads on the walls. Anything that lets us know furniture and such stays where it's put until it rots away. Speaking of rot, what's left of some draperies hang on each side of the French doors. Doom, gloom and dust. Possums in the attic. Rats in the walls. It's that sort of place. SOUND: HOWLING WIND.)*

(AT RISE: NIGHT. A couple of the lamps are LIT, casting eerie SHADOWS. Nothing for several seconds, just long enough for the audience to take in the eccentric view. The HOWLING WIND SUBSIDES. Then --)

GRANNY'S VOICE. (*From top of the stairs.*) Aeosp! What you got, Aesop? I seed you from the window. (*GRANNY comes down the stairs and INTO VIEW. She's a mountain crone who appears to be as old as the house. Her hair is long and stringy. Despite her years, she moves fast.*)

GRANNY. Be it wild turkey, mebbe? I dotes on wild turkey. (*AESOP ENTERS DOWN LEFT. He's a hillbilly lad wearing overalls and a floppy hat. He is dragging his hunting rifle behind him as if it were a child's toy. He stops when he sees GRANNY.*) Ain't a hunter in these parts good as you, Aesop. What did you fetch home? (*AESOP holds up a dead squirrel, or rabbit, by it's tail. GRANNY is unimpressed.*) That's it? Out all day and all you brung home is one puny squirrel? (*AESOP slams the carcass on the table with a THUMP. Dragging his rifle, he heads for the cellar.*) Ain't enuff to feed a starvin' kitten. How can I cook up a mess of vittles if'n all I got for the casserole is one puny squirrel? (*In way of answer, AESOP EXITS behind the cellar door, still dragging his rifle. GRANNY crosses to the squirrel and picks it up for a closer look.*) Mighty puny. Reckon Aesop's mind ain't on whut it should be. (*Shaking her head.*) 'Tain't surprisin'. Drat that Daisy Belle. (*Puts down squirrel.*)

Maybe I'll stew it and toss in some turnips and greens.

ADA'S VOICE. (*From the hallway.*) Come right in. Make yourself to home. You're goin' to like it hyar.

JUNE'S VOICE. Thank you Mrs. Dimshroud.

ADA'S VOICE. Ada. Call me Ada.

JUNE'S VOICE. Ada.

(The voice startles GRANNY. She starts to EXIT DOWN LEFT. Remembers the squirrel. She grabs it just as ADA APPEARS in the front hallway, EXITS. ADA'S a rough mountain type, domineeering. She likes things to go her way. However, at the moment, she's trying to appear ladylike and gentle. For ADA this is not easy.)

ADA. Finest house in these parts. I'll have Granny make us some sassafras tea. (*ADA stops CENTER. Roars.*) Granny! (*As if calling hogs to slop.*) Gran-Gran-Gran-nnnnnny! (*JUNE HUNGERFORD stands IN the hallway. Early twenties, pretty. She holds a suitcase. Nervously she looks about.*)

JUNE. It's an old house, isn't it?

ADA. Yup. But there's none finer in these parts. Most hill people is plain envious. I know you'll be happy hyar. Let me take that. (*ADA crosses and takes the suitcase. Indicates the settee.*) Set right down and make yourself comfortable. (*Leery about the house, but anxious to appear polite, JUNE sits. ADA puts the suitcase by the stairs, talking as she goes.*) We always have a room or two fer rent. My people have lived in this house a long, long time. Home sweet home, like they say. Got most of the conveniences. (*MOVES CENTER.*) Hooked up for electricity. No television, no telephone, though. But

Aesop's got a radio.

JUNE. Aesop?

ADA. He's my son. You'll like him. (*Roars.*) *Aesop! E-e-esop!* (*JUNE cringes, forces herself to smile. Nods at the portrait above the fireplace.*)

JUNE. Who's that?

ADA. I reckon Aesop's out huntin'. When it comes to huntin', ain't none better than Aesop Dimshroud. Comes by it natcherel.

JUNE. (*Points.*) The portrait.

ADA. (*Looks.*) That's Fowler Dimshroud. He's the one who lived here first. They called him "Mudslide" Dimshroud.

JUNE. Mudslide?

ADA. I want you to meet my husband. He'll be so pleased to meet you. (*Roars.*) *Ulysses!* (*JUNE cringes.*) *Ulysses! U-u-ulysses!* (*No response.*) I reckon he's takin' a nap. There's nothin' he likes better than takin' a nap. I'll fetch him down.

JUNE. Please don't wake him on my account.

ADA. Time he was gettin' up and about. Otherwise, he'll sleep to winter. (*Crosses to the stairs, starts up.*) That man don't nap and he don't sleep. He *hibernates.* Shouldn't be a man. Ought to be a bear. *Ulysses!* (*She's gone. JUNE looks about the room, trying to make up her mind. SOUND: CAR PULLING IN, OFF UP LEFT.*)

JUNE. It's not the Hilton, but it "might" do. (*Stands, glances at the portrait.*) Mudslide? (*Woodbox interests her. She opens it and takes out a small log. Returns it, closes lid. Next the French doors catch her eye. She crosses over. Notices the shabby drapes.*) Some new drapes wouldn't hurt.

(*She opens the French doors and cautiously steps*

outside for a look. As she does, ULYSSES COMES FROM the cellar. Dirty shirt, dirty vest, battered hat. Rope for a belt. He wears a long beard and looks as if he's escaped from a "Li'l Abner" comic strip.)

ULYSSES. That you a-callin', Ada?

GRANNY'S VOICE. That you, Ulysses?

ULYSSES. Yup. It's me. Wuz that Ada a-callin'? *(GRANNY ENTERS DOWN LEFT.)*

GRANNY. 'Course it was Ada. Who else can holler like that?

ULYSSES. She got powerful lungs.

GRANNY. Ain't been sick a day in her life thanks to my doctorin'. *(AESOP COMES FROM the cellar, stands behind his father.)*

AESOP. Whut's Maw yellin' about, Paw?

ULYSSES. Ada don't need no special reason. She yells fer the sheer pleasure of yellin'.

GRANNY. Better not let Ada hear you say that.

ULYSSES. I ain't afraid of Ada.

AESOP. Oh, yes, you are. Hahaha. *(GRANNY joins in, only her laughter sounds like a cackling chicken.)*

ULYSSES. Hush up, Aesop! Hush up, Granny! *(They keep right on laughing.)*

ULYSSES. Hush up, I say! *(JUNE backs IN. The OTHERS stare, motionless. JUNE turns, sees the Dimshrouds. She finds their staring unnerving.)*

JUNE. *(Bravely.)* Hello. *(ULYSSES, AESOP and GRANNY continue to gawk -- as if they've never seen a young woman before.)*

AESOP. *(In awe.)* Gosh. *(He steps back.)*

GRANNY. Gosh. (*She steps back.*)

ULYSSES. Gosh. (*He steps back.*)

JUNE. Gosh. (*Not knowing what else to do, she steps back.*)

AESOP. Whut you done to yourself, Daisy Belle?

ULYSSES. Hush up, boy.

AESOP. Whut I say?

ADA'S VOICE. (*From upstairs.*) Ulysses, that you down thar?

ULYSSES. 'Course it's me!

AESOP. I'm hyar, Maw. Granny, too.

ADA. (*Coming down the stairs.*) Now ain't that nice. The whole family.

AESOP. We gots company.

JUNE. (*Not knowing what else to say, pointing at French doors.*) Is that a swamp out back?

AESOP. Ain't no swamp.

ULYSSES. It's a pond.

GRANNY. Folks round hyar call it Bottomless Pond on account of it ain't got no bottom.

JUNE. (*Not knowing what else to say.*) Sounds logical.

ADA. (*Steps into room.*) Ulysses, Aesop, Granny -- I want you to meet Miz June Hungerford. From the city.

AESOP. Howdy.

ULYSSES. Howdy.

GRANNY. How do.

ADA. Ulysses, Aesop, where are your manners? What will Miz Hungerford think? Take off them hats! (*Quickly, they remove their hats. To JUNE, as she points.*) That thar be Ulysses, my husband. That be Aesop, my boy, and Granny thar be my grandmother.

JUNE. Nice to meet you. (*Audience sees someone standing outside the French doors peering in. This is JUNE'S older sister BETTY.*)

ADA. Miz Hungerford's been feelin' poorly and needs a nice long rest. City got her down. Her nerves is all frazzled. I told her we had a nice furnished room for rent. Ain't that right? (*ULYSSES, AESOP, GRANNY give no response. ADA is annoyed.*) Guess you didn't hear. I said — *Ain't that right!?* (*Quickly, afraid of ADA'S wrath, the Dimshrouds bob their heads in agreement.*)

ULYSSES. That's right, Ada —

AESOP. Whatever you say, Maw —

GRANNY. Room fer rent, yes, indeedee. Room fer rent, room fer rent —

ADA. I know you're goin' to like the room, Miz Hungerford. There's a rug on the floor, a quilt on the bed and I'll give you a quarter fer ev'ry spider you find. Ha, ha.

JUNE. Spiders? Oh, I don't like spiders.

AESOP. I do.

JUNE. I'm afraid of spiders.

ADA. I was only kiddin'. Ha, ha. (*To DIMSHROUDS.*) I said I was only kiddin'!

DIMSHROUDS. Ha, ha, ha.

ADA. The room is snug and comfy.

JUNE. I suppose it won't do any harm to look. (*BETTY steps back from French doors.*)

ADA. 'Course not. Granny, you take Miz Hungerford upstairs and show her the room we got fer rent.

GRANNY. What room is that?

ADA. (*Explodes.*) The room with the rug on the floor and the quilt on the bed!

GRANNY. Oh. That one. (*Moves for stairs. To JUNE.*) Come along with Granny. (*GRANNY starts up the stairs. JUNE moves to follow.*)

ADA. Stay as long as you like. One week, two. A whole month. If the rent's too much I can take less.

JUNE. Let's discuss it after I've seen the room.

ADA. Good idea. (*ULYSSES and AESOP continue to gawk. JUNE stares at them. They stare back. Foolishly they wave as if they were wishing her bon voyage. JUNE climbs the stairs. DIMSHROUDS watch her go.*)

AESOP. I declare. It's Daisy Belle's twin.

ADA. Hush up, you fool. You'll spoil ev'rythin'.

AESOP. Aw, Maw. You're always pickin' on me. I don't like it.

ADA. You don't, huh? I'll show you. (*Fast, she moves to the desk, picks up a whip.*)

ULYSSES. Boy's right, Ada. That gal does look like Daisy Belle.

ADA. Hush up about Daisy Belle. She might overhear.

AESOP. How can Daisy Belle overhear?

ULYSSES. Daisy Belle ain't hyar to overhear. (*ADA moves CENTER, brandishes the whip.*)

ADA. I ain't talkin' about Daisy Belle. I'm talkin' about June Hungerford. Next time either one of you menfolk sasses me back, you'll get a taste of this.

AESOP. Aw, Maw.

ULYSSES. We wasn't sassin'.

ADA. Hush up! (*With that, she snaps the whip to the floor. CRACK! ULYSSES and AESOP cower. ADA crosses to table.*) Git over hyar. (*ADA sits and, fast, AESOP and ULYSSES make for the table and sit. They talk like conspirators in the dark.*) Now lissen good. You know we won't git no quarterly check from that lawyer woman lessen she sees Daisy Belle, like always.

AESOP. What you reckon happened to Daisy Belle?

ADA. Anything could have happened to Daisy Belle. Daisy Belle was a mite purty gal, but she sure was dumb. That don't matter none. What does matter is that lawyer woman. If'n she finds Daisy Belle ain't hyar, we could be in a heap of bad trouble.

ULYSSES. We already got enuff.

AESOP. Don't need no more.

ADA. All that's important is gettin' that check.

ULYSSES. Us Dimshrouds is doomed without it.

AESOP. Mebbe someone kidnapped Daisy Belle, or mebbe she fell into Bottomless Pond when she was fishing.

ULYSSES. Ain't no fish in Bottomless Pond.

AESOP. That wouldn't matter none to Daisy Belle.

ADA. I told you to hush up about Daisy Belle. We got Miz Hungerford. Don't need no Daisy Belle.

ULYSSES. How you gonna git thay city gal to pretend she's Daisy Belle?

ADA. I'll figure out somethin' when the time comes.

AESOP. What if'n she don't want to stay?

ADA. (*Bangs whip handle on table top.*) She's got to stay.

ULYSSES. Can't force her.

ADA. First things first. I don't want no trouble from you two. As far as June Hungerford is consarned, we're jist one big happy mountain family. *Smile!* (*ULYSSES and AESOP force grins.*)

AESOP. (*Through his clinched teeth.*) How's this?

ADA. Have to do, I reckon. (*GRANNY starts down the*

stairs.)

GRANNY.   You'll be able to hear all kinds of birds. Whippoorwills, hawks, crows, woodpeckers, hootin' owls.

JUNE. (*Following down.*) Quite a change from the city.

ADA. (*Hushed tone.*) Remember, one big happy mountain family. (*AESOP and ULYSSES continue to grin. Holding the whip, ADA stands, moves CENTER.*) How did our visitor like the room, Granny?

GRANNY. She wanted to know if we had a mop and some soap and hot water. (*GRANNY comes into room, stands RIGHT.*)

ADA.   Like I told you, Miz Hungerford -- all the conveniences.

AESOP. No television, no telephone. Have to go to the general store.

ADA. Miz Hungerford is trying to git away from such things. (*To JUNE.*) If'n it's peace and quiet you want, this is the place to be. End of a lonely road with not a noisy neighbor in sight.

ULYSSES. We ain't got no neighbors. Noisy or otherwise.

GRANNY. No one to disturb you.

JUNE. (*Hesitates.*) Well ... I ...

ADA. Then it's settled.

JUNE. I'll try it for a week.

ADA. Meals come with the room.

AESOP. Granny's a great cook.

JUNE. I don't want to be any trouble.

ADA. We're delighted to have you. To tell the truth we could use the money.

ULYSSES. Times is hard for us Dimshrouds.

ADA. Hush up, Ulysses. Miz Hungerford don't want to

hear our problems. She's got her own.

AESOP. Have Granny mix you up a tonic or a potion, Miz Hungerford. She's better than any city doctor. (*JUNE notices the whip in Ada's hand.*)

JUNE. Is that a whip?

ADA. (*Looks.*) Why, so it is. (*Thinking fast.*) It belongs to Aesop. He's always leavin' it around the house. Uses it on the mule.

AESOP. We ain't got no mule, Maw.

ADA. Hush up! (*AESOP cringes. ADA moves to desk to return whip.*)

JUNE. I'm afraid I left a bag in the cafe. Careless of me.

ADA. No problem. Ulysses, you take the truck back into town and fetch Miz Hungerford's bag from the Moonglow Cafe and Gift Shop. Aesop, you take -- (*Indicates.*) Miz Hungerford's suitcase to her room.

AESOP. What room is that, Maw?

ADA. The one with the rug on the floor and the quilt on the bed!

AESOP. Oh. That one. (*He ambles to the suitcase and takes it upstairs. ULYSSES gets up and crosses for the front hall.*)

ULYSSES. What if'n someone swiped that bag from Moonglow Cafe and Gift Shop?

ADA. You'll never know unless you go thar and find out, will you?

ULYSSES. I reckon. (*He puts his hat on, EXITS.*)

GRANNY. I'd better start on supper. We ain't like most folks in these parts. We got a dinin' room. (*GRANNY crosses DOWN LEFT. Turns back as she points OFF-STAGE.*) It's in hyar.

JUNE. (*Trying for a compliment.*) I can tell the original owner liked to live well. (*Turns to portrait.*) Uh, Fowler "Mudslide" Dimshroud had, uh, good taste.

GRANNY. The original owner warn't Mudslide. It was Pumpkin Cutter. You'll find out about him sooner or later. For your sake, I hope it's later. (*She laughs insanely, EXITS.*)

JUNE. (*Uncomfortable.*) Pumpkin Cutter?

ADA. Don't pay no attention to Granny. You may not have noticed, but she's a li'l tetched.

JUNE. Tetched? (*ADA taps her skull.*)

ADA. You know -- in the head.

JUNE. Oh, you mean touched. Touched in the head. Her mind wanders.

ADA. I ain't troubled by her mind wanderin'. It's when it takes a long walk that scares me. Reckon I'd better give her a hand. Sometimes she fergits to light the stove.

JUNE. Can I help? I don't mind making myself useful.

ADA. You're a guest. You relax. Some new magazines on that table over thar. (*ADA points to the UP RIGHT CENTER table, EXITS.*)

JUNE. (*Musing.*) Tetched in the head? (*She shrugs, crosses for the magazines. She picks up one and blows dust from the cover. Checks date.*) "August, 1990." (*Puts it down, selects another. Blows dust from cover, checks date.*) "April, 1987." (*Another.*) "September, 1936." (*BETTY APPEARS at the opened French doors, looks about to ascertain her sister is alone.*)

BETTY. Psssssst. (*JUNE hears the sound, but doesn't immediately know where it's coming from.*) Psssssst. Psssssst. June. It's me. Betty. (*JUNE turns, puts the magazine back.*)

JUNE. Betty! What are you doing here?

BETTY. I'm parked out back.

JUNE. How did you find me?

BETTY. (*Steps into room, moves CENTER.*) You said you were taking a bus when you called. I went to the station and described you to the man at the ticket window. He said you were headed to this isolated town in the hills? Why?

JUNE. You shouldn't have followed me. You know very well why I'm here. *You* could have been followed. (*JUNE crosses to settee, sits. She produces a handkerchief and twists it in an absentminded fashion.*)

BETTY. I pulled into town just in time to see you driving off with that woman.

JUNE. Her name's Ada Dimshroud. She met me in the cafe and we got talking. I told her I was looking for a quiet room.

BETTY. (*Looks about.*) Quiet room? In this creepy dump? I got a brief look at the inhabitants. They make the Beverly Hillbillies seem like high society.

JUNE. Actually, the Dimshrouds are rather nice -- in a bizarre sort of way. Would you like to meet them?

BETTY. I'll take a rain check. Besides, I'm not staying and neither are you.

JUNE. Yes, I am.

BETTY. You're not making any sense.

JUNE. I'm making perfect sense. I need to hide out for a while.

BETTY. You're handling this all wrong. Simply go to the police and tell them your fiancee is in the Army, stationed in Europe. Tell them his ex-girlfriend is making your life miserable.

JUNE. She wants to kill me.

BETTY. Nonsense.

JUNE. She's threatened me several times. You know that. When she learned Bob and I are getting married, she went berserk. Followed me into the bank and started screaming that I stole the man she loved. I'm afraid of her, Betty.

BETTY. She's the emotional type. Ignore her.

JUNE. How can I? She's the one who slashed my tires. I know it. And all those strange telephone calls with no one speaking? It's Bob's ex-girlfriend. Edwina Hyde.

BETTY. Hmmmmm. I'd forgotten about those slashed tires.

JUNE. Wish I could. She's the one who sent me that funeral wreath. Had to be her.

BETTY. You're coming home with me.

JUNE. (*Hysteria building.*) No, no, no. She knows where you live. She knows where I live. She knows everything. I didn't tell you about last night. She called. She said there wasn't going to be any wedding because there wasn't going to be any bride. (*More and more excited.*) She said if she didn't do it herself she'd find someone to "get me out of the picture." Her words, Betty. "Get me out of the picture."

BETTY. June, this is serious. Go to the police.

JUNE. They'll laugh at me.

BETTY. You're coming apart. (*Without thinking, JUNE checks herself to see if she's "coming apart."*)

JUNE. Look at me. I'm so nervous I don't know what I'm doing.

BETTY. Have you written Bob or telephoned him?

JUNE. No. Of course not. I don't want him to worry. For all I know, she might do him some harm.

BETTY. He has a right to know. If Edwina Hyde has

threatened you, you can have a warrant issued.

JUNE. That wouldn't stop her. You don't know her like I do. I used to think she was nice, but now I realize that was all a mask. She's stark raving mad! And she wants to kill me. Or she's going to have someone do it for her. People will do anything for money.

BETTY. Maybe she just wants publicity.

JUNE. Publicity! (*BETTY sits beside her sister and takes her hand.*)

BETTY. Tell me what you want me to do.

JUNE. You might have done too much already. Edwina may be insane but she's clever.

BETTY. Nobody followed me.

JUNE. How can you be sure?

BETTY. Would you like an aspirin? I have some in the car.

JUNE. Don't patronize me, Betty. All I want is some time to myself. To think.

BETTY. I wish you'd take my advice and talk to the police.

JUNE. No!

BETTY. (*Hoping to calm her down.*) Maybe coming here was a mistake. I didn't know what else to do. After all, what are big sisters for?

JUNE. A little time. That's all I need, and then I'll know how to handle Edwina.

BETTY. (*Dubious.*) Well ... have it your way. I don't like it though.

JUNE. Thanks. (*AESOP comes down the stairs. The WIND HOWLS -- SOFTLY at first, but BUILDING in intensity. The LAMPS FLICKER.*) The lamps! (*She desperately grabs at BETTY for protection. Her nerves are that shot.*)

BETTY. Easy, June. It's only the wind.

JUNE. I'm so jumpy.

AESOP. Ain't nothin' to worry about with them lamps.

JUNE/BETTY.   Oh!   (*Startled by the voice, they turn UPSTAGE as AESOP ENTERS the room.*)

AESOP. Them lamps always git fidgety when the wind's high. On account of I rigged up the wires myself. That way you don't have to pay the electrical company no money. (*Looks at BETTY.*) Who she be?

JUNE. Uh, Aesop, I'd like you to meet my sister. She won't be staying. Betty, this is Aesop Dimshroud. Ada's son. (*In a gallant gesture, AESOP whips off his hat, bows.*)

AESOP. Howdy, ma'am. You be city. I can tell by the way you're dressed. (*BETTY stands.*)

BETTY. It's nice to make your acquaintance, Slop.

AESOP. 'Tain't Slop. It's Aesop.

BETTY. Sorry.

AESOP. (*To JUNE.*) You sister sure is purty. (*To BETTY.*) You married?

BETTY. Why do you ask?

AESOP. I figure it's about time I wuz gettin' hitched and settin' up.

BETTY. Settin' up?

AESOP. Gettin' a place of my own. Raise a family. (*BETTY doesn't wish to continue the conversation.*)

BETTY. All right, June. Have it your way, but promise me you'll keep in touch. I worry about you.

JUNE. I'll soon be myself again.

BETTY. I wish you'd call Bob.

JUNE. *Please!* (*BETTY can see JUNE is beyond reasoning with, and AESOP is making her uneasy.*)

BETTY. If you need anything, let me know. (*She crosses to French doors.*)

AESOP. Hey, Miz Betty.

BETTY. (*Stops, turns.*) What is it, Aesop?

AESOP. (*Points to front hallway.*) We got a front door.

BETTY. Good for you. Take care of my little sister. (*BETTY EXITS. AESOP looks after her.*)

AESOP. She's purty alright. Smart, too. I can tell. Can she cook?

JUNE. (*Twisting the hankerchief into a tight knot.*) Betty's a good cook.

AESOP. (*Steps toward settee.*) Can she cook possum?

JUNE. I doubt it.

AESOP. Thought you said she was a good cook.

JUNE. Possum's a little out of her line. (*Another GUSH OF WIND, more FLICKERING OF THE LAMPS.*) Can't you do something about the lamps?

AESOP. Not when the wind's blowin'. (*He crosses to cellar door.*) It's on a night like this that Granny always sees him.

JUNE. (*Twisting, twisting.*) Him? Who?

AESOP. (*Darkly.*) Pumpkin Cutter. (*He opens the cellar door, EXITS.*)

JUNE. Who is this Pumpkin Cutter person? Your great-grandmother mentioned him earlier. (*SOUND: CAR DRIVING AWAY, OFFSTAGE UP LEFT. JUNE realizes she's alone and is suddenly frightened by her surroundings.*) Nothing to be afraid of ... some howling wind ... some flickering lights. So what? (*Sudden BANGING at the front door.*) Auuugh! (*Startled practically out of her skin, JUNE jumps up. Again, the BANGING. JUNE moves DOWN LEFT.*) Mrs.

Dimshroud?   There's someone at the front door.   (*More BANGING.   JUNE reacts to each THUMP.   Calls DOWN LEFT.*) Mrs. Dimshroud? (*No response.*) Ada? (*Just as JUNE is about to EXIT for the kitchen, a young man, MIKE, dressed for hiking and carrying a backpack, APPEARS in front hallway.*)

MIKE. Hi.

JUNE. (*Edgy.*) Hi.

MIKE. I banged at the door.

JUNE. Yes, I heard you. I was getting Mrs. Dimshroud.

MIKE. The door opened by itself, so I figured it was okay to come in. (*He puts knapsack by the woodbox.*) Okay to put this here?

JUNE.   (*Wary.*) I suppose so. (*He crosses CENTER, behind sofa.*)

MIKE.   Nice night until the wind came up. (*There's something about MIKE that makes JUNE awfully uneasy. She seems unable to move.*)

JUNE. You've been hiking?

MIKE. Hiking through the hills.

JUNE. Where are you from?

MIKE. The city. I'm looking for someone special.

JUNE. (*Her words betray her fear.*) Someone special?

MIKE. Is something wrong? You're acting a little odd.

JUNE. Am I?

MIKE. Am I frightening you? (*He steps toward her and she, on instinct, steps in front of table and crosses to settee.*)

JUNE. You look familiar somehow. Do I know you?

MIKE. I don't think so. Name's Mike. Mike Hyde.

JUNE. (*Frantic.*) Hyde! (*Thinking she means "hide", he dives behind sofa.*)

MIKE'S VOICE.   What's wrong?   (*JUNE races for the woodbox, lifts lid, produces the small log.*)
JUNE.   People will do anything for money or publicity!
MIKE'S VOICE.   Huh?
JUNE.   Or family ties!   Blood is thicker than water.
MIKE'S VOICE.   How's that?
JUNE.   You've got a sister, haven't you?   (*MIKE flings one arm over the settee's back, and then his head COMES INTO VIEW.   He's utterly bewildered.*)
MIKE.   Matter of fact, I've got two.   Look, miss, I don't know what your problem is, but how about I go out and come in again?
JUNE.   You don't fool me.   Not for a moment.   Looking for someone special, are you?   Well, it's not going to be me.   You *assassin.*
MIKE.   Assassin?
JUNE.   (*Threatens with the small log.*)   I can protect myself. Tell that to Edwina.
MIKE.   Edwina?   (*Another RUSH OF WIND, another FLICKERING OF THE LIGHTS.   With the small log raised like a club, JUNE moves to MIKE, ready to whack him on the head..   (Arm up for protection.)*)   Hey!   What are you doing!?   (*LIGHTS BLACKOUT and JUNE hits him.   We hear a SPIRALLING DOWN GROAN.*)
MIKE'S VOICE.   *Oooooooooooooooooo* . . . .

(*When the LIGHTS FLICKER BACK ON, JUNE is discovered with the log raised over her head, looking down at the body of MIKE which is LOST FROM VIEW behind the settee.   Slowly, it dawns on JUNE that she may have done serious damage in her fear.*)

JUNE. Oh. Oh. (*She looks at the small log in her grasp. Screams. In a second or two, AESOP flings open the cellar door and ADA and GRANNY hurry IN FROM DOWN LEFT.*)
AESOP. Whut's all the commotion?
ADA. What's wrong, Miz Hungerford?
JUNE. This man ... he wanted to kill me.
DIMSHROUDS. Kill you!? (*AESOP, ADA and GRANNY quickly move behind the settee. Stunned, JUNE drops the small log and stumbles to the bench in front of the fireplace. Sits like a zombie. AESOP gets down on one knee to gauge the damage. Long pause.*)
ADA. Is he hurt bad, son?
GRANNY. Who be the varmint?
JUNE. (*In a daze.*) He wanted to ... kill ... me.
AESOP. (*Stands.*) You don't have to worry about him no more.
GRANNY. Why's that, Aesop?
AESOP. He's dead. (*JUNE stifles the scream rising in her throat.*)
GRANNY. What kilt him? (*AESOP points to JUNE.*)
AESOP. She did. (*JUNE, about to crack, jumps up.*)
JUNE. I didn't mean to! I was trying to protect myself! (*ADA crosses and puts one arm around the shaking JUNE.*)
ADA. (*Matter-of-fact.*) Now, now. Nothin' to go carryin' on about. These things happen in the hills all the time.
JUNE. They do?
ADA. You're among friends. We won't say a word. (*To AESOP and GRANNY.*) Will we? (*Pause.*)
AESOP. Nope.
GRANNY. Ain't none of our business.
ADA. What are you standin' thar fer, Aseop? Drag this

body out and dump it in Bottomless Pond. No one will ever find it thar.

AESOP. How come I always git the stoop labor.

ADA. I guess because you're stupid. No backtalk. Move! (*With a grunt of protest, AESOP takes the body by the ankles and begins to drag it toward the French doors.*)

GRANNY. I better see how my squirrel casserole is comin' along. (*Starts for DOWN LEFT, stops.*) Did I remember to skin the critter? (*She shrugs, EXITS.*)

JUNE. (*Utterly exhausted.*) I killed a man. (*JUNE sobs uncontrollably. ADA puts the other arm around the poor young woman and pats her back in motherly fashion.*)

ADA. Thar, thar.

JUNE. I'm a murderess.

ADA. None of us is perfect. (*AESOP continues to drag away the corpse. Another RUSH OF WIND and more FLICKERING FROM THE LAMPS.*)

END OF SCENE ONE

(*Burst of lively "mountain music" to cover the few seconds between scenes. Strike backpack.*)

ACT I SCENE 2

(The music carries over into the opening of this scene, fades. It's a week later.)

(AT RISE: We hear ULYSSES SINGING behind the cellar door.)

ULYSSES' VOICE. OLD DAN TUCKER, HE GOT DRUNK. FELL IN THE FIRE AND KICKED UP A CHUNK. A RED-HOT COAL ROLLED IN HIS SHOE, AND OH MY GOSH HOW THE ASHES FLEW! *(He opens the cellar door and ENTERS room. He carries a brown jug. Moves to settee, sits. He takes a swig from the jug.)*

ULYSSES. OLD MAN TUCKER WAS A FINE OLD MAN, WASHED HIS FACE IN A FRYING PAN. HE COMBED HIS HAIR WITH A WAGON WHEEL, DIED WITH A TOOTHACHE IN HIS HEEL. *(Another swig. ADA comes down the stairs in time to catch him.)*

ADA. Put down that li'l brown jug!

ULYSSES. Don't see what harm a li'l swallow kin do.

ADA. You fergittin' whut day this be?

ULYSSES. 'Course I ain't. It be Tuesday.

ADA. And what's special about this Tuesday? *(ULYSSES thinks hard, but can't come up with anything.)*

ULYSSES. How should I know? Tuesday is Tuesday. Like Monday is Monday and Wednesday is Wednesday.

ADA. Havin' faith in a husband sure is tryin'. *(Harsh.)* This be the Tuesday we git the check. That lawyer woman will be hyar any minute.

ULYSSES. Miz Spaulding.

ADA. Yes, Miz Spaulding. Miz Nose-In-The-Air Ruth Spaulding. You know we's supposed to give Daisy Belle — (*Searching for the right phrase.*) — "a healthy environment." We's supposed to set an example. How's it goin' to look if'n you're sittin' thar with a jug?

ULYSSES. You're a hard woman, Ada.

ADA. Give me that. (*She grabs the jug from ULYSSES, crosses to cellar door, opens it. Tosses in the jug. Slams the door. SOUND: JUG SMASHING.*)

AESOP'S VOICE. (*Behind door.*) *Oooooowwwwwww!*

ULYSSES. Now look whut you done.

ADA. Hush up. We got more important things to worry about. Li'l brown jug don't matter none.

ULYSSES. She gonna do it?

ADA. She'll do it. Otherwise, we might have to tell whut we know.

ULYSSES. About that stranger she kilt.

ADA. That's right. (*AESOP comes from the cellar. One hand drags his old hunting rifle and the other rubs his head. He's furious.*)

AESOP. Who threw that jug? I could have been serious hurt.

ULYSSES. Don't carry on, boy. It only hit your head.

AESOP. How'd you like it if'n your head got beaned with a jug?

ADA. Don't want no jug around when that mean lawyer shows up.

AESOP. When she gonna git hyar?

ADA. Should've been hyar by now.

AESOP. I'm goin' huntin'.

ADA. You're staying hyar. You know Miz Spaulding likes

to see the whole family. We's a unit.

AESOP. I'll stay close. (*EXITS for French doors, dragging the rifle. Rubs his head.*) Ain't right fer folks to toss jugs about like they wuz tennis balls. (*He's OUT.*)

ULYSSES. That boy's got a temper.

ADA. I kin handle Aesop.

ULYSSES. Yeah. With a whip.

GRANNY. (*Coming down the stairs.*) Looks right purty on you, Miz Hungerford. I made that dress for Daisy Belle myself.

JUNE'S VOICE. I don't know if I can do this.

GRANNY. 'Course you kin. (*GRANNY ENTERS room and steps RIGHT. ULYSSES stands and moves to bench in front of fireplace. ADA crosses to table. All this is so JUNE, impersonatindg DAISY BELLE, can "make an entrance." JUNE comes down the stairs, stands UP CENTER, feeling awkward in DAISY BELLE'S clothes. The dress or pinafore is rather outlandish, although it's obviously homespun. Much too young for JUNE. She looks like Dorothy from THE WIZARD OF OZ.*)

JUNE. (*Hesitates.*) Do I look all right?

ULYSSES. You look perfect. Why, if'n I didn't know better I'd swear you wuz Daisy Belle.

JUNE. Perhaps it would be better if I contacted the police and told them the truth. You know -- confess. (*DIMSHROUDS react, alarmed.*)

ULYSSES. No,no. You can't do that!

GRANNY. They'd put you behind bars.

ADA. You ain't fully recovered from your shock. (*DIMSHROUDS rush to JUNE and guide her to the settee. They ease her down.*)

JUNE. I don't know whether I'm coming or going.

ADA. All the more reason not to worry yourself. You don't want to do anythin' rash.

GRANNY. Them wimmin's prisons is awful places, I hear tell. They make you scrub floors day and night.

JUNE. I don't want to go to prison.

ULYSSES. We don't want you to go.

JUNE. (*Sobs.*) What's to become of me? What will Bob say when he finds out?

GRANNY. Who's Bob?

JUNE. The man I was going to marry.

ULYSSES. We ain't goin' to tell no one you kilt that stranger.

JUNE. Oooooooooh.

ADA. Hush up, Ulysses. Can't you see she's fragile. (*Sweetly.*) Now, June, it does seem since we're not goin' to tell anyone whut you done, you might do us a li'l favor.

JUNE. But it's dishonest to pretend you're someone else. Isn't it? (*DIMSHROUDS exchange an indifferent look, shrug.*) Besides, this Miss Spaulding will know I'm not Daisy Belle when she hears me speak.

GRANNY. We already thought of that. We'll say you got took with the laryngitis.

ULYSSES. All you got to do is sit whar you are and look pixilated.

JUNE. Pixilated?

GRANNY. Like you wuz a li'l strange.

ADA. Like you wuz Daisy Belle.

JUNE. I don't know how to look pixilated. I don't know how to look a little strange.

GRANNY. Then jist be yourself. (*SOUND: BANGING at*

front door. ALL react.)

ADA. Thar she be. Miz Spaulding.

JUNE. I can't do it! I can't do it!

ADA. You kin do it.

GRANNY. Think about that wimmin's prison.

JUNE. Oooooooooh. (*SOUND: MORE BANGING.*)

ADA. Take her into the kitchen 'til I call.

GRANNY. Good as done. (*She waves JUNE to follow.*)
JUNE stands, follows.)

JUNE. My life is over.

ADA. Quick, Ulysses. Look busy.

ULYSSES. Whut should I do?

ADA. Whittle some wood.

ULYSSES. Where will I git the wood?

ADA. Use your head. (*WIDOW MURK APPEARS in front
hallway.*)

WIDOW MURK. Is everyone in this house asleep? (*ABOUT
WIDOW MURK: She's an aggressive neighbor. She thinks the
DIMSHROUDS are idiots and delights in making them
uncomfortable.*)

ADA. Why, look who's hyar, Ulysses. It's our good friend
and neighbor the Widder Murk.

ULYSSES. How do, Widder Murk. (*In way of answer,
WIDOW MURK marches to the table, pulls out a chair. Sits.*)

WIDOW MURK. I've come to remind you about the money.
(*ADA and ULYSSES fawn over her.*)

ULYSSES. We ain't forgot.

ADA. How about some sassafras tea?

WIDOW MURK. Nope.

ULYSSES. Granny's made some cornbread. Pipin' hot.

WIDOW MURK. No tea. No cornbread.

ADA. You're lookin' fine and fit, Widder. Don't the Widder look fine and fit, Ulysses?

ULYSSES. Fine lookin' woman fer her age. Always said so.

WIDOW MURK. Listen to me, both of you. I know my ABC'S and I know my IOU'S. I lent you sixty thousand dollars *in cash* to pay your back taxes.

ULYSSES. That's right, Widder, and we's mighty grateful.

WIDOW MURK. But you didn't pay your back taxes.

ADA. But we will.

ULYSSES. Daisy Belle hid the money and we don't know whar.

WIDOW MURK. You should have watched the girl. You know she's peculiar.

ULYSSES/ADA. Mighty peculiar.

WIDOW MURK. You signed a document putting up this house and the surrounding land as security for the loan.

ADA. That wuz legal, warn't it?

WIDOW MURK. Perfectly legal. Let me explain something to you.

ADA. We're all ears. (*ADA AND ULYSSES quickly sit at the table.*)

WIDOW MURK. (*As if instructing backward pupils.*) If you don't pay your back taxes, the government will seize this house and the land. Since I have a *legitimate* claim, I'm sure the government and myself will be able to strike a deal. Understand?

ULYSSES. Whut's that mean?

WIDOW MURK. What I just told you!

ULYSSES. No. Legitimate.

ADA. But the government can't seize the property if'n we

pay the taxes.

WIDOW MURK. No. But you'll still owe me sixty thousand dollars, and if you don't pay up this property is mine.

ULYSSES. Mighty confusin'. We owe taxes to the government and we owe you the money you lent us to pay the taxes.

WIDOW MURK. Now you've got it.

ULYSSES. We don't want it.

ADA. The government will git it's money jist as soon as we find out whar Daisy Belle hid it. You'll git your money, Widder. We're expectin' a check today.

WIDOW MURK. I wonder what Miss Spaulding would say if she knew you were using Daisy Belle's money to pay back a personal loan?

ULYSSES. We got a right. We's her guardians.

WIDOW MURK. I've said my piece. Time's running out. That document you signed is legally binding. Be prepared for the worst. Always helps. (*SOUND: BANGING at front door.*)

ULYSSES. This time it has to be Miz Spaulding.

WIDOW MURK. (*Stands.*) I'm not anxious to see her. Can't abide the woman. She's cold. I'll go out the back. (*Crosses to French doors, OUT.*)

ADA. (*Calls after her.*) Nice to see you, Widder. (*Aside to ULYSSES.*) She's a misery. Only comes hyar to torment us. She enjoys watchin' us squirm. She hates us Dimshrouds. Always has.

ULYSSES. On account her family wuz kin to Pumpkin Cutter. Why'd we take her money, anyhow?

ADA. 'Cause she wuz the only one who'd lend us. Our financial standin' in this community ain't the best.

ULYSSES. Can't get blood from a tulip. (*SOUND:*

BANGING at front door.)

ADA.   Don't stand thar with your mouth hangin' open. Answer the door.

ULYSSES. Hot diggity! Payday. *(He hurries into the front hall. ADA fluffs at her dress and touches at her hair, hoping to make a good impression.   GRANNY ENTERS with a chamber pot of wild flowers.)*

GRANNY.   Here, Ada. Dress up the table.

ADA.   Reckon them flowers can't hurt. *(ADA takes the pot and puts it on the table. GRANNY scurries OFF, DOWN LEFT.)*

ULYSSES' VOICE. *(From front hallway.)* Sure is good to see you agin, Miz Spaulding.

RUTH'S VOICE.   Is it?   *(ULYSSES appears in front hallway.)*

ULYSSES. Here she be, Ada. Miz Spaulding. All the way from the city. *(Ulysses steps by the fireplace bench.)*

ADA.   Always nice seein' you, Miz Spaulding.

(RUTH SPAULDING ENTERS. A haughty ice queen dressed in menacing, albeit stylish, black. Latest chic hat. Gloves. She holds a handsome attache case. She absolutely abhors her assignment and finds the DIMSHROUDS repulsive. She finds it difficult to be civil.)

ULYSSES. *(Indicates settee.)* Set yourself down. Granny's got tea and cornbread.

RUTH. I won't be staying.

ADA. You never do.

RUTH. I'm a busy woman. *(RUTH steps in front of sofa.*

She puts the attache case on the floor. Produces a wide handkerchief and spreads it out on the settee. When she's certain she has a clean place to sit, she lowers herself gracefully onto the settee.) As you know, under the terms of Daisy Belle's trust, the law firm is required to deliver a quarterly check *in person.*

ADA. Like always.

RUTH. Your distant cousin, Daisy Belle's uncle, insisted.

ULYSSES. Distant cousins is the best kind.

RUTH. I can't help but believe Daisy Belle's uncle might have made other arrangements if he had visited you in his lifetime.

ADA. That don't matter none. Kinfolk is kinfolk.

RUTH. *(Frosty.)* Yes. When Daisy Belle turns thirty, all the money remaining in the trust will be turned over to her directly. You do understand?

ULYSSES. Does that mean we don't get nothin' more fer takin' care of her?

RUTH. That is so, Mister Dimshroud.

ULYSSES. How's we Dimshrouds supposedly to live?

ADA. Hush up.

ULYSSES. I got a right to ask questions! Don't tell me to hush up!

ADA. I'll show you! *(Without thinking, ADA darts to the desk and gets the whip. She moves behind the table and snaps it to the floor. CRACK! ULYSSES cowers. Obviously, MISS SPAULDING has seen this type of unorthodox behavior before. Instead of being shocked, she merely sighs.)*

RUTH. Shall we forget your impersonation of Indiana Jones and get on with matters at hand? Let me see Daisy Belle and get the ritual over with.

ADA. *Daisy Belle!*

RUTH. Must you shout?

ADA. (*Whispers.*) Daisy Belle. (*A moment passes and JUNE APPEARS from DOWN LEFT. GRANNY behind her.*)

RUTH. Ah, there you are, Daisy Belle. (*Not knowing what else to do, JUNE performs a stupid curtsy.*) You look well. Any problems? Anything I can help you with? (*JUNE shakes her head.*) In that case, I shall deliver the check and be on my way.

GRANNY. But you jist got hyar.

RUTH. (*Frosty.*) Yes. (*She picks up the attache case, opens it.*) Have you given any thought to college, Daisy Belle?

ULYSSES. How can she think about college when she ain't graduated from grade school?

RUTH. Cat got your tongue?

JUNE. (*Barely audible.*) Laryngitis.

RUTH. I beg your pardon?

DIMSHROUDS. Laryngitis.

RUTH. Laryngitis? Has she seen a doctor?

GRANNY. Daisy Belle don't need a doctor when Granny's hyar. I take good care of her.

RUTH. She does look a little pale. Perhaps she should be in bed.

GRANNY. That's a mighty fine idea. Thank you fer thinkin' of it. Miz Spaulding. Up to bed, Daisy Belle. Granny will tuck you in.

RUTH. If you need to get in touch with me for any reason, you have my telephone number, Daisy Belle. (*Not knowing what else to do, JUNE curtsies again. GRANNY pushes her into the UPSTAIRS hallway and up the stairs. RUTH takes a check from the attache case.*) Here's the check. There won't be another for another three months. (*Both ULYSSES and ADA dive for the check, but ADA gets it. She looks at it with great pleasure.*)

RUTH. (*Closes attache case, stands.*) I'll be on my way. (*Picks up handkerchief.*)

ULYSSES. You're in and out like a breeze, Miz Spaulding. (*RUTH moves LEFT of sofa, and crosses behind it.*)

ADA. Did you notice the purty flowers on the table? (*Indicates.*) We do ev'rythin' humanly possible to give Daisy Belle a good and lovin' home.

RUTH. (*Frosty.*) Yes. (*AESOP blunders IN from French doors, dragging his rifle.*)

ADA. You almost missed seeing Aesop, Miz Spaulding.

RUTH. No such luck.

AESOP. (*Steps to RUTH.*) How do, Miz Spaulding. See whut I got. (*He holds a skunk by it's tail. RUTH is aghast, screams. Bolts for the front hallway as fast as her legs carry her.*)

ULYSSES. Whut you shoot a skunk fer?

AESOP. I didn't shoot it. It's a road kill. (*He crosses DOWN LEFT, EXITS.*)

ULYSSES. I trust Granny won't put that in a casserole.

ADA. Never mind that. You take this hyar check over to Widder Murk.

ULYSSES. It's gonna take more than Daisy Belle's trust checks to pay back sixty thousand dollars.

ADA. You let me worry about that. *Move!* (*Check in hand, ULYSSES runs into the front hall and OUT.*)

AESOP'S VOICE. *Maw!*

ADA. Now what? (*SHE EXITS DOWN LEFT as GRANNY comes down stairs.*)

GRANNY. She'll be fit as a fiddle in no time, Miz Spaulding. Leave ev'rythin' to Granny. (*ENTERS room, sees that she's alone.*) Where'd ev'ryone go?

PAUL'S VOICE. (*From outside the French doors.*) Hello.

GRANNY. Hello.

PAUL'S VOICE. Hello.

GRANNY. Hello. (*PAUL sticks his head IN.*)

PAUL. Hello.

GRANNY. 'Pears to me one of us is a echo.

PAUL. You own this place?

GRANNY. Come in, come in. Can't abide it when someone's half in and half out. (*PAUL PEMBROOK ENTERS. Handsome young man. Urbane.*)

PAUL. I don't mean to intrude. Let me introduce myself. Name's Paul Pembrook. I paint.

GRANNY. My name's Granny Dimshroud and I don't paint. This house ain't been painted in over a hundred years. We Dimshrouds like it that way.

PAUL. You misunderstand. I don't paint houses. I paint pictures. Landscapes mostly. I've been hiking through these hills searching for good subjects. (*Notices portrait.*) That's interesting. May I have a look?

GRANNY. Suit yourself. That be an ancestor. (*PAUL crosses and inspects the painting with great interest as he talks.*)

PAUL. That pond outside is unusual looking. It has a vague, mysterious quality.

GRANNY. That be Bottomless Pond.

PAUL. Would you object if I painted it?

GRANNY. Why should I?

PAUL. I'd like to make a copy of the portrait too. I won't be any trouble. I promise. (*Sizes up GRANNY.*) You'd make a good subject.

GRANNY. Fer whut?

PAUL. A portrait. (*Indicates portrait.*) Like this fellow.

GRANNY. (*Delighted, flattered.*) That's a fine idea! I alway's hankered fer a paintin' of myself. Can you start now?

PAUL. I left my things in town.

GRANNY. Git 'em. If'n you gonna paint my picture, you ought to stay hyar in the house. Make it easier fer you.

PAUL. I couldn't do that.

GRANNY. 'Course you can. Ain't ev'ry day I git my picture painted. I'm offerin' you Dimshroud hospitality. "Tain't polite to refuse.

PAUL. I guess I could come back tonight and make a few preliminary sketches.

GRANNY. You do that, mister. (*PAUL crosses for French doors.*)

PAUL. These hills are a painter's inspiration.

GRANNY. Jist make sure you make old Granny look good in paint.

PAUL. Count on it. (*He EXITS. SOUND: FRONT DOOR OPENING and BANGING SHUT.*)

GRANNY. (*Turns to sound.*) Who that be?

(*Pause for impact, and then DAISY BELLE ENTERS. She wears a baggy raincoat and slouch hat. NOTE: The roles of DAISY BELLE and JUNE HUNGERFORD are, of course, played by the same actress. DAISY BELLE speaks with a hillbilly accent and, for the rest of the play, always appears wearing the baggy raincoat and the slouch hat.*)

DAISY BELLE. Howdy, Granny. I'm home.
GRANNY. (*Arms wide to welcome her.*) You're back. Oh, we wuz so worried. *Welcome home -- Daisy Belle!*

END OF SCENE TWO

(MORE LIVELY "MOUNTAIN MUSIC")

ACT I SCENE 3

(That night. A storm is brewing. SOUND OF DISTANT THUNDER. The lamps flicker, a fire glows in the hearth. The view is eerie. A few seconds prior to curtain or scene's opening, we hear the voices of the Dimshrouds, excited.)

ADA'S VOICE. It was jist one of your fancies, Granny --
AESOP'S VOICE. You wuz confused --
ULYSSES' VOICE. It wuz Miz June Hungerford you saw --
(By now we can see the DIMSHROUD clan hovered around GRANNY who is seated at the table.)
GRANNY. I tell you, I saw Daisy Belle.
ADA. June Hungerford.
GRANNY. I reckon I can tell the difference twixt Miz Hungerford and Daisy Belle.
AESOP. Whar she be then?
ULYSSES. We searched the house from top to bottom.
AESOP. Inside and out. No Daisy Belle.
GRANNY. (*Adamant.*) I know what I seed.

ULYSSES. Sure would be nice if'n Daisy Bell wuz back. She could tell us whar she hid the money.

GRANNY. She come in right after that painter fella said he wanted to paint my picture.

DIMSHROUDS. Painter fella?

GRANNY. He does landscapes mostly. (*ADA, ULYSSES and AESOP sigh. They're convinced GRANNY is imagining things. ADA makes a circle around one ear with a finger to indicate GRANNY is balmy. AESOP and ULYSSES nod agreement.*) I invited him to stay.

AESOP. And whar he be?

GRANNY.   He'll be back.   Handsome young fella. (*DIMSHROUDS give up. GRANNY plucks a flower from the pot. Smells it, and then eats it. SOUND: BANGING at front door.*)

ADA. I wonder who that be? At this hour? Go see who it is, Aesop.

AESOP. Aw, Maw. I don't like to answer the door. That's wimmin's work.

ADA. You want me to git the whip!? (*On that, AESOP bolts into the front hall and OUT.*)

ULYSSES. It's probably Widder Murk back to watch us spin on the spit. I think she give us that money jist so she can plague us whenever she wants.

GRANNY. She got Cutter blood.

ADA. She's a mean female. No doubt about that.

GRANNY. It's probably that painter fella at the door. (*AESOP thunders back IN.*)

AESOP. It's the Sheriff! (*AESOP scurries to the bench in front of the fireplace, sits. Pretends to warm his hands. The DIMSHROUDS are on guard.*)

ULYSSES. Wonder what he wants?

ADA. We'll know soon enuff. (*SHERIFF GREEN ENTERS. Holster, service revolver.*)

SHERIFF. 'Evenin', Ada.

ADA. 'Evenin'.

SHERIFF. 'Evenin', Ulysses, Granny.

ULYSSES/GRANNY. 'Evenin', Sheriff.

ADA. Whut brings you out this a-way?

SHERIFF. I hope I'm not disturbing you. I wanted to see you before the storm breaks.

ADA. (*Crosses between table and settee.*) How about some coffee, Sheriff?

SHERIFF. No thanks.

ADA. Won't you set yourself? (*She gestures to settee. SHERIFF crosses down, sits.*)

SHERIFF. Thanks. (*He takes out a note pad and flips it open.*)

ULYSSES. I hope you don't think I've been makin' corn likker down in the cellar. I don't do that no more. I be reformed.

SHERIFF. I hope so, Ulysses. You know it's against the law. Wouldn't want to have to arrest you. (*Taps note pad.*) Actually, I'm looking for someone. I'm hoping you may have seen him.

ADA. Who might that be?

SHERIFF. A college student. Name of — (*Glances at pad.*) Michael Hyde. (*Fill in the description so it matches the actor playing the role of MIKE HYDE.*) ( ) Hair. ( ) Height and weight. ( ) eyes.*)

GRANNY. Don't ring no bell.

ULYSSES. Nope.

SHERIFF. Seems he went hiking in these hills a week ago and no one's seen him since.

DIMSHROUDS. Tsk, tsk.

SHERIFF. He was a folklorist.

ADA. He was a florist?

SHERIFF. *Folk*lorist. That's a person who studies customs and beliefs. He was a college student working on his thesis.

AESOP. Workin' on his *whut?*

SHERIFF. He was observed at the Moonglow Cafe and Gift Shop and, after that, he plain disappeared. (*DIMSHROUDS remain cool.*)

ADA. What makes you think we'd know anythin' about him?

SHERIFF. No reason special. I'm asking everyone in these hills. He might have gotten lost.

AESOP. He could have been et by a bear.

ULYSSES. Fell down a mountain and cracked his skull open. Bled to death.

ADA. The snakes have been real bad this season. (*A distraught JUNE comes down the stairs.*)

JUNE.   Did I hear someone say the Sheriff's here? (*DIMSHROUDS are horrified.*)

ADA. Daisy Belle!

ULYSSES. We thought you wuz sleepin'. (*ADA crosses UPSTAGE.*)

JUNE. I can't sleep. There's too much on my mind. Sheriff --

SHERIFF. Yes, Daisy Belle?

JUNE. There's something I want to tell you.

GRANNY. She's got a fever, Sheriff. Don't let her get too close. Hill fever is contagious.

AESOP. She got the flu, too.

ULYSSES. And double laryngitis.

SHERIFF. She does look a little wobbly.

JUNE. You don't understand, Sheriff. (*ADA slaps a hand to JUNE'S forehead.*)

ADA. Why, she's burnin' up. Quick, Ulysses, we've got to get her into bed. (*ULYSSES crosses to JUNE.*)

JUNE. I don't want to sleep.

GRANNY. Hush up, gal. You don't know whut you're sayin'. (*ADA and ULYSSES push JUNE to the stairs and all three go up.*)

JUNE. (*Protesting.*) But I want to speak to the Sheriff. (*AESOP takes advantage of the distraction to slip behind the cellar door.*)

SHERIFF. You sure she's going to be all right?

GRANNY. She ain't been herself since the fever took. But I look after her good.

SHERIFF. If you do see anything of this Michael Hyde, let me know immediately.

GRANNY. We ain't got no telephone.

SHERIFF. Send Aesop into town. (*Looks for AESOP.*) Where'd he go?

GRANNY. Never know with Aesop. (*PAUL APPEARS at the open French doors carrying some painting gear -- easel, canvas, paint box. SHERIFF stands.*)

PAUL. Hi, Granny. I'm here.

GRANNY. I can see that. (*To SHERIFF.*) This be Paul Pembrook. (*Preens.*) I'm doin' some modelin' fer him. (*PAUL puts down the gear.*)

PAUL. Granny's going to be a great subject.

GRANNY. This be Sheriff Green. (*PAUL crosses over and*

the two men shake hands.)
PAUL. Sheriff.
SHERIFF. I think I've seen you in town. Been here long?
PAUL. Few days.
SHERIFF. Reason I ask -- I'm looking for a lost hiker.
Name of Michael Hyde. (*Gives physical description of the
actor playing the role, checking his note pad.*)
PAUL. I haven't seen anyone to fit that description.
SHERIFF. Keep your eyes open. I'd appreciate it.
PAUL. You bet.
GRANNY. (*Anxious to change the subject.*) I'm goin' to put
my picture up thar aside old Mudslide.
PAUL. Mudslide? (*SOUND: CRASH OF THUNDER,
LAMPS FLICKER.*)
SHERIFF. That's Fowler Dimshroud. Somethin' of a
legend in theses parts.
GRANNY. It's on account of him that Widder Murk gives
us such misery.
PAUL. Why did they call him Mudslide?
SHERIFF. Bottomless Pond out back used to be low water
with muddy banks. One day they found Fowler floating face
down. Folks figured he drank too much corn likker and lost
his balance and slid down the mud and drowned. Of course,
this was a long time back. Around 1880.
GRANNY. Fowler Dimshroud might have slid down the
mud, but that ain't how he died. (*SOUND: NEARING
THUNDER.*)
SHERIFF. Granny knows all the old stories.
GRANNY. It was Pumpkin Cutter whut come out of the
pond and pulled ole Fowler in.
SHERIFF. (*To PAUL.*) Pumpkin Cutter was the original

owner. He lost the property to Fowler in a poker game and was so distraught he drowned himself in the pond. He's supposed to haunt the water. Or so the story goes.

GRANNY. Ain't no "story." It's true. There's been a curse on us Dimshrouds ever since.

SHERIFF. (*Humoring her.*) Sure, sure, Granny.

GRANNY. Pumpkin Cutter ain't goin' to be satisfied until he drags the last of the Dimshrouds down to a watery grave. He's plain spiteful. Jist like Widder Murk.

PAUL. He sounds like a sore loser.

SHERIFF. I'll be on my way. Keep your eyes open, Mister Pembrook.

PAUL. I'll make a point of it. (*DAISY BELLE wanders IN from DOWN LEFT.*)

DAISY BELLE. Howdy, Sheriff.

SHERIFF. Hello, Daisy Belle. (*He looks UPSTAGE, and then back to DAISY BELLE.*) I thought you were sick in bed. Upstairs. (*GRANNY thinks fast.*)

GRANNY. She must have crawled out of bed and come down the back stairs into the kitchen.

SHERIFF. Why's she wearing a raincoat?

GRANNY. It's going to rain, ain't it? (*SHERIFF gives DAISY BELLE a hard stare.*)

SHERIFF. She moves fast. You sure you're all right, Daisy Belle?

GRANNY. Don't you fret, Sheriff. You know Daisy Belle and her ways.

SHERIFF. (*Still staring at DAISY BELLE.*) Nice meeting you, Mister Pembrook.

PAUL. Same here. (*SHERIFF EXITS.*)

GRANNY. This be distant kin, Mister Pembrook. He's

goin' to paint my picture, Daisy Belle.

DAISY BELLE. Paint my picture, Mister Pembrook.

GRANNY. I'm goin' to tell the others you're back agin. Keep an eye on her, Mister Pembrook. Don't let her out of your sight.

PAUL. I'll do my best. (*GRANNY moves UPSTAGE. AESOP comes crashing through the French doors.*)

AESOP. Granny! Granny! I seed him!

GRANNY. Where'd you git to, Aesop?

AESOP. I can't deal with no lawman. Never mind about that. I seed him. Rising up from the mud and headin' this way.

PAUL. Who? (*AESOP gives a quick look over his shoulder.*) *Here he comes!*

(*AESOP runs up the stairs and OFF. EFFECTS GO WILD. THUNDER, FLICKERING LIGHTS. ALL look to the French doors. A HORRIBLE APPARITION, like Frankenstein's creature, ambles a few steps into the room. DAISY BELLE screams and runs OUT, DOWN LEFT. ABOUT THE APPARITION: His hair is covered with weeds and his old clothes are draped with vines. The eyes are blacked out and his skin color is ghoulish. He's clotted with gore. Because of the SHADOWY LIGHT, we can barely make him out. He looks like something dragged up from the depths of the Bottomless Pond.*)

PAUL. (*Horrified.*) What on earth? (*GRANNY turns aside and holds up one arm as if to ward off the evil presence. She stamps her foot to emphasize her terrified words.*)

GRANNY. Go away! Go away! Don't look, Mister Pembrook. He's got the evil eye. It's him! It's him!
PAUL. Who?
GRANNY. *Pumpkin Cutter!*

(With his arms outstretched as if to embrace GRANNY, the APPARITION ambles a few stiff-legged steps forward, making a guttural sound. The LIGHTS BLACKOUT. There's a CRACK OF THUNDER and a FLASH OF LIGHTNING at the French doors. The only light in the room is the GLOWING FIRE in the hearth.)

GRANNY. *Pumpkin Cutter! Pumpkin Cutter! Back from his watery grave!*

END OF ACT I

ACT II SCENE 1

(The following day.)

(AT RISE: GRANNY is seated CENTER on one of the chairs from the table. She sits in profile, hands folded in her lap. She looks like Whistler's Mother. PAUL has his easel set up close by, palette and brush working.)

PAUL. Not getting tired, are you, Granny?

GRANNY. I never git tired. 'Pears to me the light in hyar ain't too good fer paintin'.

PAUL. I don't want direct light. I'm after shadow and mood. Texture. I'm painting you in dark colors because I see you at something from another time, another place.

GRANNY. Ain't that somethin'. *(Pleased.)* I'm from another time, and another place.

PAUL. Hold your head still. *(Checks the pose.)* Good. Excellent. *(SHERIFF ENTERS via French doors.)*

SHERIFF. I looked the pond over good. I couldn't find anything. I'm used to granny saying she's seen the ghost of Pumpkin Cutter. But this is the first time someone else has seen it.

PAUL. *(Puts palette on table.)* I don't know if I saw a ghost, Sheriff. I certainly saw *something*.

SHERIFF. Let me get this straight. Some intruder came into the house and gave you a scare.

PAUL. A good scare. I was frightened. I admit it. That's enough for today, Granny.

GRANNY. Suit yourself. *(GRANNY gets up, positions the*

chair back at the table.)

SHERIFF. (*Crosses behind settee.*) Anyone else see this, uh, ghost?

PAUL. No, just Granny and myself. (*Recalls.*) Wait a minute, Daisy Belle. Daisy Belle saw the ghost. Aesop, too. Only I don't think it was a "ghost." Maybe a tramp or psycho. An escaped lunatic.

SHERIFF. Escaped from where? (*JUNE comes down the stairs.*)

PAUL. I have no idea. Where do lunatics usually escape from?

GRANNY. Oh, it were a fierce sight Sheriff Green. Wish you could of bin hyar.

SHERIFF. I hate writing these reports.

GRANNY. (*Melodramatic.*) His eyes wuz all sunk in and his skin was moldy and his hair wuz all messed up. There wuz pond scum and such all over him. I reckon he's powerful lonely down thar at the bottom of the pond.

SHERIFF. That pond's not supposed to have a bottom.

GRANNY. Then mebbe he jist floats in the watery mud. Floats and stays lonely. (*SHERIFF is doing his best not to lose his temper. He thinks all this Pumpkin Cutter stuff is rubbish.*) JUNE stands UP CENTER.)

SHERIFF. Uh,yeah,well.

JUNE. (*Weakly.*) Hello.

GRANNY. Daisy Belle! (*PAUL and SHERIFF turn UPSTAGE.*) You ain't supposed to be out of bed.

SHERIFF. I'd like to ask you a few questions, Daisy Belle.

JUNE. (*Sleepily.*) Questions?

SHERIFF. Tell me what you saw.

JUNE. When?

SHERIFF. Last night.

JUNE. I didn't see anything last night. (*GRANNY rushes to JUNE'S side.*)

GRANNY. Don't upset her, Sheriff.

SHERIFF. You didn't see some creep walking about this place?

JUNE. No.

GRANNY. (*Hand to JUNE'S forehead.*) She's half out of her head with the fever.

JUNE. (*Nods at PAUL.*) Who's this?

GRANNY. This is Mister Pembrook. He's paintin'my picture. Say's I'm from another place and another time.

SHERIFF. I'll buy that.

JUNE. Sheriff.

SHERIFF. Uh-huh.

JUNE. Sheriff, what's the penalty for murder in this state?

SHERIFF. Murder? We got the death penalty. (*JUNE half-faints.*)

JUNE. *Ooooooooooooo.* (*GRANNY struggles to hold her up. PAUL quickly crosses over and helps.*)

PAUL. I've got her, Granny.

GRANNY. Whut you have to go and say that fer, Sheriff?

SHERIFF. What I say?

GRANNY. Death penalty.

SHERIFF. She asked me, didn't she?

JUNE. I'm all right.

PAUL. Sure?

JUNE. Yes. Thank you. (*JUNE recovers.*)

SHERIFF. Mister Pembrook, I don't know what kind of game you're playing, but I don't appreciate it.

PAUL. I'm not playing any game.

SHERIFF. My time is valuable.

PAUL. So is mine. Look, someone came crashing in here last night and he looked *dangerous.*

SHERIFF. He came in and gave you a scare, and then turned around and went back out?

GRANNY. That's right.

SHERIFF. Why didn't you go after him, Mister Pembrook?

PAUL. You can't be serious? He might have had a gun or a knife. I'm no hero.

GRANNY. He disappeared in the storm.

SHERIFF. Makes you wonder why he bothered to come in in the first place.

GRANNY.   All them Cutters delights in tormentin' us Dimshrouds.

SHERIFF. I don't appreciate getting my leg pulled. As far as I can tell, no crime has been committed. I'll be back. I'm keeping my eye on you, Mister Pembrook.

PAUL. It's a free country.

GRANNY. Mister Pembrook knowed what he saw. He don't lie. He's a gentleman.

JUNE. Sheriff, are you sure?

SHERIFF. About what, Daisy Belle?

JUNE. Murder. It's a death penalty.

SHERIFF. I'm sure. It's my job to know. (*Suspicious.*) You sound different somehow, Daisy Belle.

GRANNY. (*Fast.*) It's the triple laryngitis clearin'up. (*SHERIFF fixes JUNE with a hard stare.*)

SHERIFF. Mister Pembrook --

PAUL. Yes?

SHERIFF. If you see Pumpkin Cutter again, tell him I'd like a few words. (*EXITS into hallway. We hear him laughing uncontrollably.*) Hahahahahaha!

PAUL. He didn't believe us, Granny.

GRANNY. None so blind as them whut won't see.

JUNE. I think I'd better lay down. Whatever you gave me last night, Granny, it's made me very weak.

GRANNY. 'Tweren't nothin' but a li'l potion to help you sleep. You need another glass. Shouldn't be up and about askin' questions of the Sheriff. You need to conserve your strength.

JUNE. (*Yawns.*) I am sleepy.

GRANNY. Upstairs we go. (*GRANNY guides JUNE up the stairs.*)

PAUL. Need any help?

GRANNY. I can manage. (*PAUL goes back to the easel and looks at the canvas. Picks up the brush and makes a small adjustment.*)

PAUL. That's better. (*SOUND OF FRONT DOOR OPENING AND SLAMMING SHUT. In a monent, a frantic BETTY ENTERS.*)

BETTY. I want to see my sister. Where is she? (*PAUL puts the easel and canvas against the UPSTAGE wall, LEFT.*)

PAUL. I don't work here. I paint here.

BETTY. Aren't you a Dimshroud?

PAUL. I've been accused of a lot of things, but never that.

BETTY. May I sit down? (*Without waiting for a reply, BETTY sits on the settee.*) I apologize if I seemed curt.

PAUL. No problem.

BETTY. I've been so worried about my sister.

PAUL. Your sister?

BETTY. June Hungerford. Is she all right?

PAUL. I've only been here one night, but I haven't met

anyone by the name of June Hungerford.

BETTY. She's here. I hope.

PAUL. Just the Dimshrouds and a late night visitor from the local stagnant pond.

BETTY. Sorry?

PAUL. Forget I said anything. (*He crosses behind the settee.*) Name's Paul Pembrook.

BETTY. Betty Hungerford. I hope she hasn't left and gone somewhere else. She's not herself at all. Very impulsive.

PAUL. You want me to get Mrs. Dimshroud?

BETTY. I'd appreciate it. Thank you. (*AESOP comes from the cellar.*)

AESOP. (*Joyful.*) I de-clare! You're back.

BETTY. Hello, Slop.

AESOP. *E-sop.*

BETTY. I keep forgetting. Sorry. Aesop.

AESOP. I know why you're back.

BETTY. Where is she, Aesop? My sister?

AESOP. You're back on account you like me.

BETTY. I try to like everyone. I'm easy to get along with.

AESOP. I could tell you wuz all fired up when I mentioned gettin' hitched. I figured you didn't say nothin' on account of you be the shy type.

BETTY. (*To PAUL.*) He's demented. You misunderstand, Slop, er, Aesop. I'm here to see my sister.

AESOP. I'm goin' upstairs and comb my hair and put on some pomade. When I come down we kin sit on the porch and do some courtin'. Paw's goin' to be mighty impressed when I tell him I'm hitchin' up with a city gal. (*He crosses for the stairs.*)

BETTY. No, please wait. Aesop. (*AESOP bolts up the

stairs.)

PAUL. That's a man in a hurry.

BETTY. He's impossible. Would you see if you can find Mrs. Dimshroud?

PAUL. Leave it to me. (*He crosses DOWN LEFT and OUT. BETTY stands and paces back and forth.*)

BETTY. I'll never forgive myself for leaving June in this awful place. What could I have been thinking of?

DAISY BELLE'S VOICE. (*Approaching French doors.*) SHE'LL BE COMIN' ROUND THE MOUNTAIN WHEN SHE COMES
SHE'LL BE COMIN' ROUND THE MOUNTAIN WHEN SHE COMES
SHE'LL BE RIDIN' SIX WHITE HORSES
SHE'LL BE RIDIN' SIX WHITE HORSE
SHE'LL BE RIDIN' SIX WHITE HORSES WHEN SHE COMES. (*DAISY BELLE ENTERS via French doors.*)

DAISY BELLE. Howdy.

BETTY. June! Thank goodness. (*She crosses to Daisy Belle and pulls her to the settee.*) Now don't argue and don't interrupt. This is important. (*Notices the baggy raincoat.*) I don't think that's attractive. I haven't seen that before, have I? Doesn't do a thing for you. Sit down, June. (*DAISY BELLE sits, smiles. BETTY paces.*)

BETTY. I should have listened to you. That crazy Edwina Hyde showed up at my apartment looking for you. She did everything but froth at the mouth.

DAISY BELLE. Howdy.

BETTY. She said she knew where you were and she was going to kill you. After she left I didn't waste any time. I headed straight for the hills.

DAISY BELLE. Howdy.

BETTY. When I got here I realized I did exactly what she wanted me to do. I've led her right to her victim. There's not a moment to lose. Don't bother to pack. We're gettin' out of here right now and heading for the nearest forest ranger.

DAISY BELLE. I said howdy.

BETTY. (*Without thinking.*) Howdy. (*Frowns.*) What's all this howdy business? Oh, I understand. You're "blending in" with the hills. Camouflage. I'm afraid your impersonation won't fool Edwina Hyde. You were so right. She's clever. (*BANGING at front door.*)

DAISY BELLE. Someone's at the door.

BETTY. (*Alarmed.*) Yes, yes.

DAISY BELLE. I better see who it be. 'Tain't polite to let folks stand outside.

BETTY. Stop talking that way. It's not necessary with me. (*DAISY BELLE starts to get up. BETTY pushes her back.*) Are you crazy! Don't you know who that might be? Edwina Hyde. Open that door and you're dead. You stay put. I'll deal with her. (*BETTY crosses into the front hallway. DAISY BELLE gets up and wanders OUT the French doors as GRANNY comes down the stairs.*)

GRANNY. That tonic ought to make her sleep for hours. I give her three tablespoons. Locked the door, too. (*Catches sight of DAISY BELLE EXITING.*) Daisy Belle! Daisy Belle! Ev'rybody's bin lookin' fer you. (*She steps to the French doors and EXITS. PAUL ENTERS DOWN LEFT. ADA is behind him.*)

PAUL. Here's Mrs. Dimshroud. (*No BETTY.*) That's odd. She was here a moment ago. She was anxious to see you.

ADA. Well, she ain't hyar now.

PAUL.   Said she was looking for her sister.   Someone named June Hungerford.

ADA.   (*Evasive.*)   Never heard the name.   She must have come to the wrong place.

PAUL.   I guess if it's really important she'll be back.

ADA.   I reckon.   You ain't had no breakfast, Mister Pembook.   I'll fix you some.

PAUL.   I feel I should be paying for my room and board.

ADA.   You're makin' Granny feel mighty happy.   I say that's fair exchange.   'Sides, we're going to git the picture, ain't we?

PAUL.   I promised Granny.   I can always paint another for myself.   I've made sketches.

ADA.   'Course if'n you want to pay somethin' I won't refuse.

PAUL.   Good.   (*Points to portrait.*)   I wish I could paint as well as the man who painted that portrait.

ADA.   Coffee's on the stove.   (*ADA turns, EXITS.   PAUL FOLLOWS.   GRANNY RETURNS.*)

GRANNY.   Drat that Daisy Belle.   Never stays put long enuff to be caught.

BETTY'S VOICE.   (*From hallway.*)   I don't live here, you understand.

ISABEL'S VOICE.   Maybe someone else can help us.

DORIS.   I hope.   (*BETTY ENTERS followed by two college girls.   ISABEL WARD and DORIS FINLEY.   They wear hiking gear.*)

GRANNY.   If'n you're lookin' fer rooms, we's full up.

BETTY.   I'm here for my sister. June Hungerford.

GRANNY.   Oops!

BETTY.   (*Looks about.*)   June?

ISABEL. Are you by any chance, Granny Dimshroud?

GRANNY. (*Wary.*) Who you be?

ISABEL. (*Steps into room.*) My name is Isabel Ward and this is Doris Finley.

GRANNY. You be hikin' through the hills?

DORIS. (*Steps into room.*) That's right.

GRANNY. I be Granny.

DORIS. Great.

ISABEL. You see, a friend of ours came looking for you and he never came back.

DORIS. The police have him down as a missing person.

GRANNY. Why was he lookin' fer me?

ISABEL. He's a folklorist.

GRANNY. Oops.

DORIS. Working on his thesis. He told us he was going to Granny Dimshroud's cabin because she knew more about these hills than anyone alive.

GRANNY. That's true. I be famous in these parts. But I give up the conjurin'.

ISABEL. Did he come here?

GRANNY. Nope. Sheriff already bin askin'.

DORIS. Something strange must have happened to him.

BETTY. Do you think he met with foul play?

ISABEL. Mike knew how to take care of himself. He was sort of a wilderness man.

DORIS. Since the police haven't come up with anything, we thought we'd trace his steps. Figure out where he might have hiked.

ISABEL. The only thing for sure is that he planned to meet Granny Dimshroud.

GRANNY. Well, he didn't and that's that.

BETTY. Do you have a picture?

DORIS. With a newspaper clipping. (*She produces it, hands it to BETTY.*)

ISABEL. It's a long article about strange mountain customs and ways. Mike wrote it.

BETTY. I remember reading this. My sister pointed it out. Front page.

DORIS. We had some classes with Mike. You can't imagine how upset everyone is.

BETTY. Here, Granny. You take a look. (*BETTY crosses over and holds out the newspaper clipping to GRANNY. She barely glances at it.*)

GRANNY. Nope. Ain't never seed him. (*Anxious to shift the topic.*) You college gals into that folklore stuff?

ISABEL. Yes, both of us.

DORIS. It's our major. Anthropology.

GRANNY. You come with me down into the root cellar and I'll show you my fascinatin' herb garden. (*Crosses for cellar door.*) 'Tain't no ordinary herb garden 'cause ev'rythin' I got is special. Elephant garlic, squaw tea, peppergrass. (*She EXITS.*)

ISABEL. She's a classic mountain type, isn't she?

BETTY. (*Crosses over.*) You noticed.

DORIS. She certainly didn't want to talk about Mike.

BETTY. (*Returns clipping.*) No, she didn't. I wonder where my sister's gone? She's not herself at all.

ISABEL. Did you get the feeling Granny Dimshroud knew more than she was telling?

BETTY. Believe me, anything's possible in this squirrel cage.

DORIS. I don't know why, but I have the strangest feeling

Mike's been here.

ISABEL. You're imagining things.

DORIS. Maybe. (*GRANNY sticks her head out the cellar door.*)

GRANNY. You want to see my fascinatin' special herb garden or not!?

DORIS. Yes.

ISABEL. We're coming, Granny.

BETTY. Let's get her talking. We may find out something. (*They EXIT into cellar. ULYSSES ENTERS DOWN LEFT.*)

ULYSSES. Didn't know we had company.

BETTY. You, you. (*He looks over his shoulder as if she were talking to someone else.*)

ULYSSES. You talkin' to me?

BETTY. Of course I'm talking to you. You're Mister Dimshroud, I presume.

ULYSSES. Always have been.

BETTY. Where is my sister?

ULYSSES. Who be your sister?

BETTY. (*Exasperated.*) *June Hungerford.*

ULYSSES. (*Reacts.*) Never heard of her.

BETTY. I'm staying the night. I am not leaving without my sister.

ULYSSES. All the rooms is took.

BETTY. (*Produces wallet.*) You'll just have to make room for me.

ULYSSES. You won't like it hyar. All the beds is lumpy.

BETTY. Doesn't matter. I doubt if I'll be sleeping.

ULYSSES. Food's not so good.

BETTY. Fine. I'm on a diet. Just so we understand one another -- I *know* my sister is here. I don't want any trouble, but I am not leaving without her. How much is the room?

ULYSSES. Five dollar.

BETTY. (*Amazed at the low fee.*) For one night?

ULYSSES. No, fer the week.

BETTY. I won't be staying the week. (*Holds out the bill.*) Here. (*ULYSSES crosses and takes it.*)

ULYSSES. (*Looks at the bill.*) This hyar be fifty dollar.

BETTY. So?

ULYSSES. I'll see if'n Ada's got change. (*He starts to EXIT, turns back to get another look at BETTY.*)

BETTY. I'm still here. I'm not leaving. (*ULYSSES nods, EXITS.*) Oh, where could she have gone? She's driving me crazy. (*AESOP thumps down the stairs. He's wearing an old frock coat and an old top hat.*)

AESOP. Hair's combed and the pomade's on. I smell good and I'm feelin' frisky.

BETTY. (*Irritated.*) Oh, no. Not you again. (*AESOP poses STAGE CENTER.*)

AESOP. I took these duds out of Paw's old trunk. It's whut he wore when he married Maw. I figure I'll wear this coat when we git hitched.

BETTY. I have no intention of marrying you.

AESOP. I like a city gal with lots of spirit. (*He crosses to the flowers on the table and takes them from the chamber pot.*) Hyar. From me to you.

BETTY. I don't want them.

AESOP. They's a token of my affection.

BETTY. I don't want a token of your affection. I am not marrying you. (*He grabs her arm.*) Let go of my arm, you Neanderthal.

AESOP. Is that whut I am?

BETTY.   That and more.   (*He pulls her to the front hallway.*)

AESOP. You ain't foolin' me, Miz Betty. You like to play hard to git. I like that in a city gal.

BETTY. (*Slapping at him.*) Let go of me, I say. Let go.

AESOP. We can sit on the front porch and spark.

BETTY. Let go! (*They're OUT. ULYSSES RETURNS with the money bill. He hears BETTY shouting "Let go!" He crosses to the hallway.*)

ULYSSES. It wuz like I figured. Can't make no change. (*As he crosses, the APPARITION/MIKE ENTERS from the French doors and repeats the business from the end of Act One. That is -- making a guttural sound and holding his arms outstretched as if to grab at ULYSSES. NOTE: At this appearance, the audience can clearly see that it's MIKE HYDE in hideous makeup and clothing. That's okay. He stumbles a few steps forward. ULYSSES turns from the hallway and crosses for DOWN LEFT.*)

MIKE. Auuuugh. Auuuuuugh. Auuuuugh.

ULYSSES. (*Without looking up.*) Sorry. We're all filled up. If you're lookin' fer a room, try the motel next to Moonglow Cafe and Gift Shop. (*He EXITS, leaving a very discouraged "ghoul" ONSTAGE.*)

END OF SCENE ONE

(*MOUNTAIN MUSIC TO BRIDGE.*)

ACT II SCENE 2

(Later. Few moments prior to scene's beginning, we hear Daisy Belle softly singing "She'll be comin' round the mountain" and the anxious voices of the Dimshrouds.)

DAISY BELLE'S VOICE.
SHE'LL BE COMIN' ROUND THE MOUNTAIN WHEN SHE COMES
SHE'LL BE COMIN' ROUND THE MOUNTAIN WHEN SHE COMES
ADA'S VOICE. Daisy Belle, try to concentrate --
AESOP'S VOICE. It's important --
GRANNY'S VOICE. Mighty important --
ULYSSES. We need your help --

(AT RISE: DAISY BELLE is discovered seated at the table. GRANNY also sits. ULYSSES, ADA and AESOP hover.)

DAISY BELLE. Whut you need help fer?
ULYSSES. The money, Daisy Belle.
DAISY BELLE. Money?
ADA. Concentrate, gal.
ULYSSES. The money the Widder Murk gave us to pay the government.
AESOP. Fer back taxes.
DAISY BELLE. Money don't do nothin' but cause trouble.
ADA. We need that cash money, Daisy Belle.
AESOP. We done tore this house apart.

GRANNY. Looked ev'rywhar.

ULYSSES. I even tore up the floorboards.

ADA. Did you bury it?

DAISY BELLE. Nope.

ULYSSES. Didn't burn it in the fireplace, did you?

DAISY BELLE. Nope.

AESOP. Mebbe she et it.

DAISY BELLE. Nope.

GRANNY. Then whar did you hide it? (*DAISY BELLE ignores the questions.*)

DAISY BELLE. Don't you want to know whar I've bin?

ULYSSES. 'Course we do.

DAISY BELLE. I got on the bus and went to the city and I played a video game and I ate in a Chinese restaurant and I saw the same movie six times. It wuz a Walt Disney.

ADA. Wanderin' off like that. No tellin' what might have happened to you.

DAISY BELLE. Mebbe if'n I took a walk by myself I could remember whar I hid the money. I like bein' by myself.

ULYSSES. That's a good idea. You take yourself a long, nice walk. Anythin' you want.

ADA. Try to remember. Try hard.

DAISY BELLE. I will. (*DAISY BELLE smiles vacantly. Stands, EXITS via French doors. They watch her go.*)

ADA. I de-clare. A glow worm is brighter than Daisy Belle.

ULYSSES. I sure hope she recollects.

GRANNY. What are we goin' to do about the other one?

ADA. June Hungerford. I think the Sheriff already suspects somethin'.

AESOP. I'm gettin hitched. (*No reaction.*)

ULYSSES. If'n June Hungerford tells whut she done, we'll be arrested too.

GRANNY. Why? We didn't kilt no one.

ULYSSES. We's whut they call accessories before, durin' and after the factory.

ADA. If'n she makes trouble, Granny kin give her some more of that sleepin' potion.

ULYSSES. Can't keep her groggy and locked up forever.

ADA. I'll think of somethin'.

AESOP. I'm gettin' hitched. (*No reaction.*)

ADA. Aesop, you git outside and keep an eye on Daisy Belle. Don't want her gettin' lost agin'.

AESOP. Aw, Maw.

ADA. You want I should get the whip?

AESOP. You're always pickin' on me. I don't get no respect. (*He crosses to the French doors.*) I'm gettin' hitched. (*He waits for a reaction. There isn't any. He EXITS.*)

GRANNY. Reckon I better see whut them college gals is up to down in the root cellar.

ADA. They're snoopers.

GRANNY. They knew all about me. I be famous.

ADA. If'n we don't find that money, bein' famous won't matter. Leave them college gals to me. I'll git rid of them. (*She EXITS DOWN LEFT.*)

ULYSSES. If'n it ain't one thing it's another. (*He crosses UPSTAGE, up the stairs.*)

GRANNY. I wonder why we didn't take a check from the Widder instead of cash? Would have made things simpler. (*She EXITS DOWN LEFT. DORIS and ISABEL cautiously open the cellar door and step out, on guard. DORIS has MIKE'S backpack from Act I, Scene 1.*)

DORIS. We've got to report this to the police.

ISABEL. How'd Mike's backpack get into the cellar?

DORIS. They were hiding it, of course.

ISABEL. What do you think they did with Mike?

DORIS. I don't like to think about it. Let's go. (*SHOCK EFFECT: MIKE jumps up from behind the settee.*)

MIKE. *Boo!*

DORIS/ISABEL. *Auuuugh!*

MIKE. It's only me. (*He climbs over the back of the settee and plops down. DORIS and ISABEL are wide-eyed.*)

DORIS/ISABEL. *Mike!*

MIKE. Shhhhhhh.

DORIS. (*Confused.*) What's all this?

ISABEL. Those clothes, that ghoul getup.

DORIS. Is this your idea of a joke?

MIKE. They think I was murdered. The Dimshrouds. I was knocked out, that's all. Good size bump on my head. They tossed me in the pond. I suppose they thought I'd sink to the bottom. Anyway, I thought it would be a great opportunity for a "field experiment."

ISABEL/DORIS. Field experiment?

MIKE. I'd see how primitive types react when they came face-to-face with a living superstition. I'm pretending to be Pumpkin Cutter.

DORIS. They tried to murder you?

ISABEL. Don't you think you ought to see a doctor? Or the police?

MIKE. The ghost of Pumpkin Cutter is a local legend. The reaction I'm getting will be a big part of my thesis.

DORIS. You got a reaction from us. You always were a prankster, but aren't you carrying things too far?

MIKE. Education should be fun. I'm enjoying myself.

ISABEL. You would. If you only knewhow upset everyone is.

DORIS. Mike, I'm really angry at you. (*AESOP ENTERS via French doors.*)

AESOP. Howdy. (*He crosses for DOWN LEFT.*)

DORIS/ISABEL. (*Mumbling.*) Howdy.

MIKE. (*Sotto. To Girls.*) Watch. (*He goes into his ghoul "act." Lifts both arms as if to strike someone down.*) Auuuuuuugh! Auuuuuuugh! Auuuuuuugh!

AESOP. (*No reaction, except --*) Don't I know you? (*Pause.*) You look like someone I seed before. But who? (*BETTY comes down the stairs.*)

BETTY. Aesop, is that you?

AESOP. (*Boasts.*) She be my intended. (*Not wanting BETTY to see him, MIKE steps behind DORIS and ISABEL. BETTY doesn't notice.*)

BETTY. (*Steps into room.*) Aesop, there are several locked rooms upatsirs. I would like the keys, please.

AESOP. You'll have to ask Maw.

BETTY. Where is she?

AESOP. In the kitchen, I reckon. (*He EXITS DOWN LEFT. BETTY crosses after him.*)

BETTY. I want to see what's in those rooms. I won't take no for an answer. (*She's OUT.*)

DORIS. Who's she?

MIKE. This place gets a lot of traffic.

ISABEL. You didn't scare that fellow.

MIKE. Interesting type. (*Front door SLAMS.*) Someone's coming.

(He slips behind the cellar door. In a moment, EDWINA HYDE BURSTS INTO the room. She holds a revolver at the ready. She marches behind the settee. She's in a vengeful mood, that's easy to see. Jumpy, almost hysterical.)

DORIS. She's got a gun! *(Fast, EDWINA turns. Sees DORIS and ISABEL. EDWINA is about BETTY'S age and everything we've heard about her is true. No one steals the man she loves and gets away with it.)*
EDWINA. Who are you?
ISABEL. Who are you?
DORIS. *(Hands up.)* Please don't shoot.
ISABEL. We're innocent college students.
EDWINA. Where is she? Don't try to protect her.
DORIS/ISABEL. Who?
EDWINA. Don't play innocent. *(MIKE slips INTO VIEW.)*
MIKE. Take it easy, lady. You don't want to shoot anyone. We're all friends here.
EDWINA. You look terrible. You ought to get some sun.
MIKE. Who is it you're looking for?
EDWINA. June Hungerford. *(Looks UPSTAGE.)* Probably upstairs.
DAISY BELLE'S VOICE. *(Approaching French doors.)*
SHE'LL BE COMIN ROUND THE MOUNTAIN WHEN SHE COMES
SHE'LL BE COMIN ROUND THE MOUNTAIN WHEN SHE COMES ... *(DAISY BELLE ENTERS.)*
DAISY BELLE. Howdy.
EDWINA. *Aha!* There you are, June.
DAISY BELLE. I'm not June. I'm Daisy Belle.

EDWINA. What a laugh.

MIKE/ISABEL/DORIS. (*Yelling to DAISY BELLE.*) Run! She's got a gun! She's going to shoot you! (*OPTIONAL SOUND EFFECT: EDWINA actually FIRES a shot. Whether she does or doesn't, DAISY BELLE spins around and EXITS.*)

EDWINA. (*Calls after her.*) Run as fast as you want! You're not getting away from me! Once I sink my teeth in, I don't let go. (*Spins around.*) You three. (*Indicates cellar door.*) Get in there and don't come out until I say so. Otherwise -- (*She makes a threatening gesture with the weapon. In a panic, DORIS, ISABEL and MIKE quickly DISAPPEAR behind the cellar door. EDWINA crosses to it and turns the key in the lock.*) One peep out of any of you and you'll get what June Hungerford's going to get.

VOICES. (*Behind door.*) Okay, okay. (*EDWINA takes a deep breath and crosses for the French doors.*)

EDWINA. Adios, Miss June Hungerford. (*She moves for the French doors. As she does, we hear the front door SLAM and the VOICES of RUTH SPAULDING and WIDOW MURK.*)

RUTH'S VOICE. It's an absolute outrage!

WIDOW MURK'S VOICE. I thought you would want to know. (*EDWINA EXITS.*)

RUTH'S VOICE. You did the right thing. (*RUTH ENTERS, followed by WIDOW MURK. RUTH looks furious and WIDOW MURK looks smug.*)

RUTH. Mrs. Dimshroud! (*Nothing.*) Mrs. Dimshroud!

WIDOW MURK. Maybe they're not here.

RUTH. More than likely they saw the car drive up and ran off. Mrs. Dimshroud! (*ULYSSES comes down the stairs.*)

ULYSSES. Well, I de-clare. It's Miz Spaulding. Howdy, Miz Spaulding. Howdy, Widder.

RUTH. This isn't a social call.

WIDOW MURK. Better fetch Ada.

ULYSSES. Sure, sure. Happy to. (*Leery of the visit, ULYSSES crosses DOWN LEFT, OUT.*)

RUTH. There may be grounds for legal action.

WIDOW MURK. Taking advantage of that poor sweet Daisy Belle.

RUTH. I intend to put a stop to that. (*She crosses in front of the settee. Produces a handkerchief, spreads it out so she can sit. She sits primly, lips pressed together.*)

WIDOW MURK. (*Steps LEFT of sofa.*) It's an awful family. Always has been.

RUTH. There's no need to remind me. I have long advised my partners that the law firm should do everything possible to remove Daisy Belle from this bizarre atmosphere. I'm only one lone voice howling in the wilderness.

WIDOW MURK. You've got them in the bear trap now. What Ulysses did is illegal, isn't it?

RUTH. It's certainly unethical.

WIDOW MURK. If this town could get rid of the Dimshrouds, it would do a lot for the ecology.

RUTH. You hate them, don't you?

WIDOW MURK. I'm only thinking of Daisy Belle.

RUTH. Yes, yes. Quite right. The issue is Daisy Belle. (*ADA ENTERS, wiping her hands on an apron. ULYSSES and GRANNY stand in the dining room entryway.*)

ADA. Ain't this a nice surprise.

RUTH. Is it?

ADA. How about a glass of lemonade? I made it fresh.

RUTH. Mister Dimshroud, please step in here. (*He does, sitting at the table. GRANNY scurries to the rocker, sits.*) I've asked the Sheriff to meet me here.

ADA. Sounds mighty serious.

RUTH. It is. Where's Daisy Belle?

GRANNY. Out somewhere. Thinkin'.

RUTH. About what?

GRANNY. Some money she hid.

WIDOW MURK. (*To RUTH.*) The money I lent them for the taxes, no doubt.

RUTH. Which is why I'm here. (*Produces check. Holds it up.*) Do you recognize this check?

ADA. (*Crosses, takes check. Looks.*) It's the one you give us. It's our quarterly. (*BETTY ENTERS from DOWN LEFT. She holds a large metal ring from which dangle several keys. She's swiftly checking them one by one as she moves UPSTAGE. ADA, ULYSSES and GRANNY have their attention glued to the check. AESOP is behind BETTY. He's disturbed that she has the keys.*)

AESOP. Maw! Maw!

ADA. Hush up, Aesop.

AESOP. (*Pointing to BETTY as she EXITS up the stairs with the keys.*) But Maw, you don't understand.

DIMSHROUDS. Hush up, Aesop!

AESOP. But Maw.

ADA. Only one way to deal with you, boy. (*Fast, she crosses to the desk and pulls out the whip.*) When I say hush up, I mean -- hush-up! (*She cracks the whip to the floor. Crack! Everyone except RUTH reacts, jumping a little. ADA puts the whip on the table.*) Aesop's a good boy, but he needs trainin'.

RUTH. Mister Dimshroud, is that your "X" on the back of the check?

ADA. (*Looks.*) 'Course it's his "X." I'd recognize his "X" anywhar. He always makes it real small. (*AESOP moves to desk.*)

ULYSSES. Almost dainty.

RUTH. You gave that check to Mrs. Murk as partial payment for a personal loan. Is that correct? (*PAUL ENTERS via front hallway. He has a canvas and his paint box.*)

GRANNY. It's Mister Pembrook.

PAUL. Am I interrupting something?

GRANNY. Jist some misunderstandin' about a check.

RUTH. More than a misunderstanding, I'm afraid. (*PAUL puts the paint box and canvas UP LEFT of front hallway. He's curious about the powwow. Stands quietly, trying to appear as unobtrusive as possible.*)

ADA. Whut you drivin' at, Miz Spaulding? How'd you get that check?

WIDOW MURK. I gave it to Miss Spaulding.

ULYSSES. How come?

WIDOW MURK. I felt it was my duty as a good citizen.

ULYSSES. Thought you didn't like her.

ADA. I wish someone would tell me what the problem be.

RUTH. The problem be -- (*Catches herself.*) The problem is this. The money that check represents can only be used for one purpose. The care and boarding of Daisy Belle. It's her money, not yours. You cannot use her money for your own purposes.

ADA. If'n we can't pay with Daisy Belle's checks, this property goes to the Widder. Or the government fer back taxes.

RUTH. That's none of my concern.

GRANNY. It's the Pumpkin Cutter curse. That's what it is.

WIDOW MURK. You might go to jail for this.

ADA. Widder Murk, you're a sly vixen. You took that check and never said nothin'.

GRANNY. So she could use it agin' us Dimshrouds. (*SHERIFF ENTERS from front hallway.*)

SHERIFF. 'Evenin', all.

RUTH. Ah, Sheriff, there you are. I was explaining the situation to the Dimshrouds.

SHERIFF. Like I told you, Miss Spaulding, I'm sure they didn't have any criminal intent. Are you sure you want to press charges?

RUTH. I'll have to consult with my law firm. In any case, I consider these people unstable and I want you here for protection.

DIMSHROUDS. Unstable?!

AESOP. We ain't got no stable.

RUTH. This is not a fit residence for Daisy Belle. I'm taking her with me. The law firm is the trustee. For better or worse.

GRANNY. Takin' Daisy Belle away from the hills?

ULYSSES. She loves the hills.

ADA. She belongs hyar.

RUTH. That check says it all.

AESOP. Checks can't talk.

SHERIFF. Aren't you a little harsh?

RUTH. It's for Daisy Belle's own good.

DAISY BELLE'S VOICE. (*Approaching French doors.*)
SHE'LL BE COMIN' ROUND THE MOUNTAIN WHEN SHE COMES
SHE'LL BE COMIN' ROUND THE MOUNTAIN WHEN SHE COMES --

ALL.   It's Daisy Belle! (*ALL look to the French doors.
DAISY BELLE ENTERS.*)

ADA.   Daisy Belle, did you remember whar you hid the
money? (*DAISY BELLE steps into the room.*)

DAISY BELLE.   I didn't hide it.

WIDOW MURK.   Daisy Belle, Miss Spaulding is taking you
away.

DAISY BELLE.   I don't want to go anywhere. I like it here.
The hills is home.

ADA.   Thar. What did I tell you?

SHERIFF.   Daisy Belle, this money the Widder lent. If you
didn't hide it, what did you do with it?

DAISY BELLE.   I took it with me.

SHERIFF.   Took it with you?

DAISY BELLE.   To the city.

ADA.   Sixty thousand dollars?!

ULYSSES.   In cash!

RUTH.   Good heavens.

DAISY BELLE.   I spent some. For the video game and the
Chinese restaurant and the Walt Disney movie. Don't forget I
seed it six times.

ADA.   But whar's the money?!

DAISY BELLE.   I got it right hyar. (*Pats the pocket of the
raincoat.*)

PAUL.   The raincoat? (*She dips her hands into the pockets
and takes out fistfuls of bills which she tosses into the air. The
money flutters down like feathers.*)

DAISY BELLE.   Whee! (*Following action is fast. As soon
DAISY BELLE says "Whee" and tosses the money, she runs
OUT the French doors. OTHERS ignore the fluttering bills and
rush after her, frantically yelling, dialogue overlapping.*)

DIMSHROUDS. No, Daisy Belle, no --
WIDOW MURK. That's my money --!
RUTH. Stop her --!
SHERIFF. Come back, Daisy Belle --
AD LIBS. Stop! Come back! Catch her! (*Etc.*) (*As they EXIT, DAISY BELLE runs back IN from DOWN LEFT. She runs CENTER, stops. Faces audience and tosses more bills into the air.*)
DAISY BELLE. *Whee!*

(*In a moment, OTHERS pour IN from DOWN LEFT and rush for DAISY BELLE. BLACKOUT. The LIGHTS FLASH ON and the OTHERS are frozen in running position as they supposedly give chase. The effect is like a "stop action" on film. BLACKOUT. LIGHTS FLASH ON and DAISY BELLE is standing by the front hallway entry, money in hand, frozen in place. OTHERS are in various static poses -- running, arms outstretched. One foot in the air. The funnier the better. BLACKOUT. LIGHTS FLASH ON and DAISY BELLE is on the stairs. OTHERS caught in the action of running to the stairs. BLACKOUT. LIGHTS FLASH ON and DAISY BELLE is standing CENTER. OTHERS surrounding her in static poses as if to grab. Hold for a moment. DAISY BELLE is happy with all the excitement she's causing. She's smiling. NOTE: If you wish to add some fast CHASE MUSIC to this sequence, it will prove effective. DAISY BELLE unfreezes and tosses more money about. The OTHERS stand motionless. Into her pockets go her hands and out come fistfuls of bills. Into the air they go and, again they flutter down.*)

DAISY BELLE. *Whee!*

(*She runs OUT the French doors. BLACKOUT. This time when the LIGHTS FLASH ON, everyone is on their hands and knees gathering up the money. As soon as the DIMSHROUDS have collected as much as they can, they deposit it in a pile on the table.*)

ADA. Sixty thousand dollars and she wuz walkin' round with it.

ULYSSES. In the city!

AESOP. 'Tweren't hid at all.

SHERIFF. Hold it, folks. (*ALL stop, look to SHERIFF.*) Isn't going to help with everyone going loco. Leave the money where it is. (*OTHERS stand.*)

ADA. I'm sure we got enuff fer them taxes. (*Positions at this point should be roughly: DIMSHROUDS at the table. PAUL by the fireplace bench. RUTH and WIDOW MURK in front of the settee. SHERIFF CENTER.*)

WIDOW MURK. What if you do? This property will come to me because you'll *never* be able to repay my loan.

RUTH. Certainly not with any of Daisy Belle's money. (*BANGING behind cellar door.*)

ISABEL'S VOICE. Open the door!

DORIS' VOICE. Let us out.

SHERIFF. Now what?

GRANNY. Sounds like them college girls. (*PAUL steps to the door and turns the key. DORIS and ISABEL stumble out.*) Who locked you gals in?

DORIS. It was some crazy lady.

ISABEL. With a gun.

OTHERS. Gun?

SHERIFF. Do you know who she was?

ISABEL. No. But she meant business.

DORIS. She was looking for someone named June Hungerford.

DIMSHROUDS. Oops.

ISABEL. And she chased after someone named Daisy Belle.

RUTH. Daisy Belle! (*JUNE is coming down the stairs with BETTY.*)

JUNE. I'm all right, I tell you. A little sleepy, that's all.

BETTY. We've got to get away from here.

SHERIFF. There's Daisy Belle now.

ADA. (*To ULYSSES.*) How'd she get loose?

AESOP. That's whut I wuz tryin' to tell you. My intended took the keys. (*ALL look UPSTAGE. JUNE and BETTY ENTER room.*)

BETTY. Sheriff, I want to prefer charges against these people. They've been keeping my sister prisoner and I suspect they've drugged her. (*DIMSHROUDS exchange a worried look.*)

JUNE. Sheriff, I have a confession to make. (*On tiptoes the DIMSHROUDS start to sneak OFF, DOWN LEFT.*)

SHERIFF. Where do you think you're going? Stay right there. (*DIMSHROUDS freeze, slowly turn.*)

WIDOW MURK. She looks like Daisy Belle, but she doesn't sound like Daisy Belle.

JUNE. I'm not Daisy Belle. I'm June Hungerford and I killed a man. I murdered Michael Hyde. (*General reaction.*)

ADA. It whar self-defense. (*SHERIFF takes JUNE by the

*arm, guides her onto the settee. RUTH and WIDOW MURK
step aside.)*
RUTH.   (*Out to the audience.*) Does any of this make
sense?
SHERIFF. You don't look so good. Sit here and tell me that
again.
JUNE. It's simple, really. I'm getting married next month
to a serviceman stationed in Europe and his ex-girlfriend has
been hounding me.
BETTY. Threatening my sister's life. She's a mental case.
PAUL. Obviously, the woman these girls saw with a gun.
(*Nods to DORIS and ISABEL.*)
JUNE. I came here to hide out, but she sent her brother to
kill me.
SHERIFF. What did you do with the body?
ISABEL. (*To JUNE.*) Boy, do you have a surprise coming.
DORIS. You, too, Sheriff.
SHERIFF. How so? (*The cellar door FLINGS open and
MIKE jumps out giving his best "ghoul" performance yet. He
looks horrific. Hands up like claws about to tear. ALL react,
in shock.*)
MIKE. *Auuuuugh!*
GRANNY. He's back! Pumpkin Cutter! (*DIMSHROUDS
yell and dash OUT, DOWN LEFT. RUTH and WIDOW
MURK scream and dash into the front hallway and OFF,
absolutely terrified. SHERIFF pulls out his service revolver.*)
SHERIFF. (*To MIKE.*) Get those hands on your head.
MIKE. (*To JUNE.*) You only thought you killed me.(*Rubs
off some of the ghoulish makeup.*) I'm no ghost.
DORIS. (*Critical.*) He wanted to see what kind of reaction
he could get.

ISABEL. For his thesis on local folklore.

SHERIFF.   I said get those hands on your head. (*DIMSHROUDS creep back INTO VIEW.*) Half the county looking for you.

MIKE. I didn't mean any harm.

JUNE. Any harm? All this time I thought I was a murderess!

BETTY. Poor kid. Sheriff, you're going to arrest someone, aren't you?

SHERIFF. As soon as I find out what the crime is. (*He scratches his head.*)

AESOP. Now I knowed whar I seed him before.

GRANNY. You ain't Pumpkin Cutter?

MIKE. Nope.

SHERIFF. How many times I got to tell you -- hands on your head.

MIKE. Okay, okay. (*To JUNE, hands on his head.*) Incidentally, neither of my sisters are named Edwina.

SHERIFF. All of you stay right here until I get back. (*Nods to MIKE.*) I'm taking him in.

PAUL. What's the charge?

SHERIFF. I'll think of something. You better come along, Miss Hungerford.

BETTY. She hasn't done anything.

SHERIFF. She assaulted this young man, didn't she?

MIKE. What if she did, I'm not preferring charges.

SHERIFF. *Someone* is guilty of *something.* We'll sort this out down at my office. You, too, Ada. Ulysses. (*EDWINA APPEARS at the French doors like an avenging angel. She has the gun in her hand and she's nearly out of control.*)

EDWINA. No one's going anywhere until I finish my work.

BETTY. (*Aghast.*) Edwina!

JUNE. *Hyde! (OTHERS hear "Hide" and dive for cover. BETTY runs UPSTAGE, DIMSHROUDS drop behind the table. PAUL slips into the front hallway. DORIS and ISABEL DISAPPEAR behind the cellar door. MIKE flattens himself by the bench. SHERIFF drops his gun and hits the floor behind the settee. Convinced this is it, JUNE covers her ears, closes her eyes, and steels herself for the fatal gunfire. Thus, only EDWINA is standing. Slowly, she advances on the quivering JUNE.*)

EDWINA. I've been waiting for this moment. You'll never steal another woman's boyfriend.

JUNE. (*Teeth chattering.*) I didn't steal Bob.

EDWINA. You did, you did.

SHERIFF'S VOICE. Drop that gun, miss, or I'll shoot. (*He rises from behind the sofa, service revolver at the ready. However -- it's not his revolver he's holding. It's a feather duster. In grabbing for the weapon he dropped, he's mistakenly grabbed the duster.*)

GRANNY. (*Head up.*) That ain't a gun you're holdin', Sheriff. It's my old feather duster. (*Horrified, SHERIFF realizes this is so.*)

SHERIFF. Darn. (*He stoops for his revolver.*)

EDWINA. Pick up that gun and you'll end up in a zipper bag. (*ADA stands, takes the whip from the table. A step toward JUNE.*) Thought you could get away with it, huh?

ADA. *Ah, hush up. (With that, she snaps the whip to the floor with a hard Crack. Startled, EDWINA drops the gun on impulse.*)

EDWINA. My gun! (*She stoops to pick it up, but SHERIFF is too fast for her. He retrieves his own weapon, points it at*

EDWINA. OTHERS stand or guardedly RETURN.)

SHERIFF. Leave that gun right where it is. Put your hands on you head. (*EDWINA reluctantly complies. SHERIFF steps to her. Holsters his gun and slams on handcuffs.*)

EDWINA. You shouldn't be arresting me. You should be arresting her. (*Nods to JUNE.*) She's the guilty party. She's the one who should be arrested. Thief! Thief!

BETTY. Are you all right, June?

JUNE. I've had better days. All I want to do now is see Bob.

EDWINA. Bob! Bob! He's mine! He belongs to me!

SHERIFF. (*Shoves her into front hallway.*) Let's go.

EDWINA. She's the one! She's guilty. She took him away from me. Arrest her! I demand that you arrest her. Thief! (*They're OUT.*)

BETTY. June, pack your things. We're getting out of this asylum.

JUNE. Gladly. (*Both BETTY and JUNE cross UPSTAGE and up the stairs.*)

ULYSSES. What a day, what a day.

MIKE. Look, Granny, maybe this isn't the right time. But can I have an interview with you?

GRANNY. Why not? You can stay hyar if you want. Thar's goin' to be a vacant room. It's got a rug on the floor and a quilt on the bed.

MIKE. *Fan*-tastic. I'll tell Doris and Isabel. (*EXITS into cellar.*)

ADA. (*Moves CENTER.*) Daisy Belle is back and we got the money fer them taxes, but I reckon we lose the house and ev'rything to Widder Murk. Hard times is staring us in the face. (*DIMSHROUDS look sad, hang their heads.*)

PAUL. (*Steps behind the settee.*) Is it possible you don't realize what you've got here?

ADA. Whut you talkin' about, Mister Pembrook? (*He points to the portrait.*)

PAUL. That portrait of Mudslide.

ULYSSES. Whut about it?

PAUL. It's an original John Singer Sargeant.

OTHERS. No.

PAUL. Yes. It's authentic. No doubt about it.

OTHERS. Who's John Singer Sargeant?

PAUL. A famous American portrait painter. One of the best.

GRANNY. You reckon I can pose for him?

PAUL. I don't think so, granny. He's been dead a long time. I recognized the style immediately and the signature. Didn't you ever check the signature? (*DIMSHROUDS shake their heads.*) That portrait is worth a small fortune. (*DIMSHROUDS react.*)

DIMSHROUDS. Fortune?!

PAUL. You can return that money to Widow Murk, pay your taxes and have plenty left over.

ULYSSES. We's saved!

AESOP. I can't wait to tell my intended.

ADA. You ain't foolin' with us, Mister Pembrook?

PAUL. Trust me. I know that portrait's worth. (*DAISY BELLE, still wearing raincoat and slouch hat, trots down the stairs, steps into the room.*)

DAISY BELLE.

SHE'LL BE COMIN' ROUND THE MOUNTAIN WHEN SHE COMES

SHE'LL BE COMIN ROUND THE MOUNTAIN WHEN

SHE COMES -- (*OTHERS, delighted with their good luck, join in.*)
   ALL.
SHE'LL BE RIDIN' SIX WHITE HORSES
SHE'LL BE RIDIN' SIX WHITE HORSES
SHE'LL BE RIDIN' SIX WHITE HORSES WHEN SHE COMES. (*GRANNY scoops up money from the table and tosses it into the air.*)
   GRANNY. *Whee!*

END OF PLAY

PRODUCTION NOTES

ON STAGE: Settee or sofa, table with 2 chairs, stool. Key in cellar door, bench, fireplace, firewood box with small log. Portrait of 19th Century gent, 2 small tables with lamps, old magazines, French doors with rotted drapes. Desk with whip and lamp. Rocking chair.

Additional stage dressing as / if desired: Grandfather clock, carpet or rug(s), rustic chandelier, framed family photos, stuffed animal heads, etc.

BROUGHT ON, ACT I, SCENE 1: Floppy hat, hunting rifle, dead squirrel or rabbit (stuffed toy) (AESOP), suitcase (JUNE), battered hat, long beard (ULYSSES), hanky (JUNE), backpack (MIKE).

BROUGHT ON, ACT I, SCENE 2: Little brown jug (ULYSSES), hunting rifle (AESOP), Daisy Belle's dress or pinafore (JUNE), chamber pot with wild flowers (GRANNY), attache case with check, hanky (RUTH), skunk (toy) (AESOP), baggy raincoat, slouch hat (JUNE).

BROUGHT ON, ACT I, SCENE 3: Note pad, holster, service revolver (SHERIFF), easel, canvas, paint box (PAUL).

BROUGHT ON, ACT II, SCENE 1: Easel, canvas, palette, brush (PAUL), newspaper clipping (DORIS), wallet with money bill (BETTY), old frock coat, top hat (AESOP).

BROUGHT ON, ACT II, SCENE 2: Mike's backpack (DORIS), apron (ADA), check (RUTH), metal ring with keys (BETTY), canvas, paint box (PAUL), many money bills (DAISY BELLE), feather duster (SHERIFF).

SOUND: Howling wind, car pulling in and out, banging at front door, mountain music, jug smashing. Storm effects -- thunder, lightning. Optional gunshot. JUNE whacks out MIKE during the blackout: to create a "whack" sound, all she has to do is hit the back of the settee or the floor with the log.

COSTUMES: As indicated in script. However, special attention should be given to the DIMSHROUDS. They should look as rustic as possible. Like ULYSSES, AESOP might have a long beard. Also, work on something truly horrific when MIKE impersonates the "ghost of Fowler 'Mudslide' Dimshroud." His clothing should look mud-covered and his make-up and hair should make him look like a ghoul.

PACING: Nothing will harm a farce more than a slow pace. The play must *move*. No dead spots. Something is always happening. Pick up cues and make entrances and exits fast. The mountain music between scenes should last only a few moments. In the original production, a banjo was used to play "She'll Be Comin' Round The Mountain."

MISCELLANEOUS: Although one actress plays both roles (JUNE/DAISY BELLE), be sure to list them separately in the program. The role of DAISY BELLE can be played by a fictional "Georgina Spelvin." Naturally, it would make a great effect if ADA could crack the revolver from EDWINA'S hand instead of cracking the whip to the floor, but this bit of business is left to the director. Role of PAUL PEMBROOK, with minor line changes, can be switched to a female role, if desired: PAULA PEMBROOK.

Also by
Tim Kelly...

The 3½ Musketeers
The Amazing Adventures of Dan Daredevil
The Butler Did It
The Butler Did It Again
The Butler Did It, Singing
The Canterville Ghost
Captain Fantastic
The Comedian
Country Gothic
The Crazy, Mixed Up Island of Dr. Moreau
Creeps By Night
Destiny
Dirty Work in High Places
Don't Be Afriad of the Dark
Frankenstein
Great All American Musical Disaster
The Great All-American Disaster Musical
The High School That Dripped Gooseflesh
Horror High, or It Came From...
Hound of the Baskervilles
How To Get Rid of a Housemother
If Sherlock Holmes Were a Woman

It Was a Dark and Stormy Night
Laffing Room Only
The Last of Sherlock Holmes
Loco-Motion, Commotion...
Love is Murder
Merry Murders at Montmarie
Money, Power, Murder, Lust, Revenge...
Murder in the Magnolias
My Son Is Crazy, But Promising
Nashville Jamboree
Night of the Living Beauty Pageant
Sherlock Holmes and the Giant Rat of Sumatra
Small Wonder
The Soapy Murder Case
That's the Spirit
Trick or Treat
The Trouble with Summer People
What's New at the Zoo?
While Shakespeare Slept
Yankee Doodle

Please visit our website **samuelfrench.com** for complete descriptions and licensing information.

OTHER TITLES AVAILABLE FROM BAKERS PLAYS

THE BUTLER DID IT, SINGING

Book by Tim Kelly
Music by Arne Christiansen
Lyrics by Ole Kittleson

5m / 5f / optional chorus

This is a delightful, audience pleasing, one-set, musical spoof based on Mr. Kelly's enormously popular hit *The Butler Did It*. Miss Maple, a flaky society dowager, invites a pack of zany detective writers to a spooky house on an isolated island and forces them to impersonate their fictional sleuths. For entertainment, she arranges some "classic" touches — a hairy face at the window, the threat of an escaped lunatic, no communications with the outside world. What she did not arrange was the body on the sitting room carpet! It's up to seedy Chandler Marlowe to solve the bizarre case and he makes a side-splitting mess of it! Ultimately, everyone has a guilty secret to confess and the real killer turns out to be the least suspected.

The happy score is dotted with likeable and show-stopping hits: "Murder, Mystery and Mayhem," "The Moth to the Flame," "Cherchez La Femme," "I Know My Stuff," and, of course, "The Butler Did It," among others. Production demands are extremely modest and the cast of ten can be expanded if desired.

OTHER TITLES AVAILABLE FROM BAKERS PLAYS

MURDER AT THE GREY'S HOUND MANSION

Maxine Holmgren

3m, 5f / Mystery, High School/ Community Theatre / Simple set

This is a mysterious comedy (or a comical mystery) that will have everyone howling with laughter.

The eccentric owner of Grey's Hound Mansion has been murdered. The cast gathers at the gloomy mansion for the reading of the will. Lightning lights up the stage as thunder and barking dogs greet the wacky characters that arrive. Each one is a suspect, and each one suspects another. Mixed metaphors and alliterations will have the audience barking up the wrong tree until the mystery is solved.

OTHER TITLES AVAILABLE FROM BAKERS PLAYS

MURDER WITH GRACE

Leon Kaye

5m, 5f / Dark Comedy, High School/ Community Theatre / Simple set

Set in the early 19th century, *Murder with Grace* tells the story of Grace, who is horrified when her brother is betrothed to Naomi, a shallow, silly girl whom Grace cannot stand to be around. She is loath to think that Naomi will soon be her sister-in-law, and so she and her good friend Beth devise a plan to manipulate Naomi by convincing her that another, much more affluent, young man named Henry is interested in marrying her. They set the plan in motion before they have actually met Henry, and it works too well–when Grace finally meets Henry, she falls head over heels for him! To make matters worse, Henry returns Naomi's attentions! It seems that Grace's only alternative would be to murder the wretched girl – that would not be very mannerly...but what alternative does she have? A dark comedy that will have even the most stoic of audiences in giggles.